BOSS OF ATTRACTION

FORBIDDEN
BOOK 3

KIMBERLY KNIGHT
RACHEL LYN ADAMS

No portion of this book may be reproduced, scanned, or distributed in any print or electronic form without permission.

This book is a work of fiction and any resemblance to any persons, living or dead, places, events or occurrences, is purely coincidental. The characters and storylines are created from the author's imagination or are used fictitiously. The subject matter is not appropriate for minors. Please note this novel contains profanity, explicit sexual situations, and alcohol consumption.

BOSS OF ATTRACTION

Copyright © 2024 Kimberly Knight and Rachel Lyn Adams

Published by Kimberly Knight and Rachel Lyn Adams

Cover art © Indie Sage

Cover Image Photographer © Wander Aguiar

All rights reserved.

NOTE FROM THE AUTHORS

Dear Readers,

Boss of Attraction makes several references to Fallon and Rhett from *Secrets We Fight* (Forbidden, #2). While this book mainly takes place after Fallon and Rhett's story ends, you can learn more about their relationship by reading SWF before or after BOA to answer any questions you may have.

Happy reading,

KIMBERLY KNIGHT
RACHEL LYN ADAMS
where love always wins

1

Sean

Five Years Ago

"This is it, isn't it?" I asked, barely able to push the words past my lips.

Julie squeezed my shoulder, a look of sympathy on her face. "We can't say for sure, but the signs are there."

Closing my eyes, I prayed for the strength I would need to continue on without the woman who had held my heart for nearly twenty-five years. And I prayed that I would be strong enough to help our son and daughter deal with their grief. It was the moment I'd been dreading since the doctors had explained there was nothing else for them to do to treat Melinda's aggressive breast cancer, and she chose to spend the time she still had at home with her family. That was six weeks ago, and it appeared my wife was ready to find some peace.

It had been four years since Melinda had received her initial diagnosis and begun to fight bravely, while undergoing chemotherapy and surgeries to try to beat the disease. Three years ago, our family had celebrated when she was told she was cancer-free, only for it to return with a vengeance. She had endured so much during her courageous battle, and after many sleepless nights and tearful conversations, during which she had shared her final wishes, I knew she was ready to let go.

"I need to call my kids." I reached for the phone in my pocket.

"If you want, I can do that for you," Julie offered.

Pressing on my son's contact, I shook my head. "No, they should hear from me. Can you sit with Melinda until I'm done?"

Julie nodded. "Of course."

She entered the bedroom and closed the door behind her, while I leaned against the wall in the hallway and lifted the phone to my ear. It only rang twice before the call connected.

"Dad?" he answered. I could hear the tremble in his voice.

It was the same way Ryan answered the phone every time I called since his mom had gotten sick again, like he was waiting for the worst to happen. Unfortunately, it appeared that time had come.

"Hi, Son. You should head over here as soon as you can."

I heard him let out a deep breath. "Okay, I'll be right there."

As soon as we hung up, I made the same call to my daughter, Morgan.

"Hi, Dad." Her voice was just as apprehensive as her brother's had been.

"Hey, sweetheart." I closed my eyes, fighting back the tears. "You need to come home."

A muffled sob came across the line. "I'm on my way."

While waiting for my son and daughter to arrive, I returned to Melinda's bedside. Julie excused herself so I could have some privacy with my wife, and I took a seat to be close to her and hold her hand. The only source of light was a lamp in the corner, which cast a faint yellow glow throughout the room. Soft music from a playlist I'd made played from a small speaker on the bedside table. As one song ended and another began, I recognized it immediately. The opening notes of "Truly, Madly, Deeply" by Savage Garden had tears filling my eyes as the memories of us dancing to it on our wedding day came flooding back.

The two of us had met during our third year of college at a party at her sorority house when we were only twenty-one-years old. The moment I saw her, I was struck by her beautiful smile and how she laughed like she didn't have a care in the world. After I found the courage to approach her, we spent the entire night talking. I remembered her sweet laugh and how she captured my heart immediately. From that moment on, we were inseparable.

It didn't take long for me to know she was the one, but we both agreed to wait until after I completed school to take the next step in our relationship. Despite our best intentions, fate had other plans, and we found out Melinda was pregnant with Ryan during my first year of law school. We decided to get married right away, and while it may have been sooner than either of us planned, we never regretted the way things turned out.

While listening to the music, I watched her breathing change, and each shallow breath served as a reminder that our time together was ending.

Stroking the back of her hand with my thumb, I whispered. "Honey, our kids will be here soon."

She didn't squeeze my hand or give any sort of sign that she heard me, but I held onto the hope that while she wasn't able to communicate, she knew I was there with her.

I had lost track of time when a small knock on the door startled me. Slowly, it pushed open, and I watched Ryan and Morgan walk in. A look of fear and vulnerability was etched on both of their faces. While they were adults, it was difficult not to see them as little kids in that moment as they approached the bed. I knew they feared losing their mother, and my heart ached for them. For all of us.

Ryan reached forward, taking Melinda's other hand in his own. "Hey, Mom," he choked out, his voice trembling. "It's me, Ryan."

Morgan stepped next to her brother, her eyes welling up with tears. "Hi, Mom," she whispered, her voice barely audible. "It's Morgan."

The three of us watched as the woman who was our entire world lay there peacefully with her eyes closed, her chest rising and falling with each shallow breath. She looked so fragile and delicate, and I hated how I couldn't do anything to heal her.

"We're here with you." Morgan hugged her mother. "We love you."

Ryan nodded, his face tearstained as well. "You've been the best mom anyone could ever ask for."

As I listened to my children shower their mother with love, I couldn't help but feel a wide range of emotions wash over me. Proud of the incredible individuals Ryan and Morgan had become, shaped in no small part by Melinda's guidance. And sadness because, in just a short time, they would be forced to say goodbye to the woman who had been their anchor throughout their entire lives.

Several hours went by as we reminisced about all the wonderful times we shared, but eventually, Melinda took her last breath, surrounded by the people who loved her more than anything, and I knew nothing would ever be the same.

A WEEK LATER, I WAS IN MY LIVING ROOM WITH MY BEST FRIEND AND former law partner, Patrick Donnelley, and his wife, Mary. Melinda's funeral and reception had ended, but I'd asked them to come back to my house for drinks.

Patrick and I had met at the first law office we worked at after graduating law school twenty years prior and became instant friends. At the time, Ryan was two-years-old, Melinda was pregnant with Morgan, and Mary was expecting their triplets—Fallon, Faye, and Finnegan. Our wives bonded right away as young mothers with husbands who worked long hours trying to jumpstart their careers, and the four of us practically raised our children together. We even spent yearly vacations together until the kids were in college.

Eventually, Patrick and I started our own law firm and we continued to work together until he left to enter politics a couple of years ago. Still, we had all remained extremely close, and they had been a tremendous support while Melinda was sick.

We sat in silence for a little while, all of us grieving in our own way. Patrick sat next to me on the couch, his fingers wrapped around a glass of whisky. His usual boisterous laughter and quick wit were absent, replaced by a solemn expression on his face. Mary sat across from us in an armchair, her eyes filled with sadness.

"Sean, I can't imagine what you're going through right now," Patrick said, his words gentle. "But please know Mary and I are here for you and the kids. Whatever you need."

I nodded, grateful for his words because I knew they would do whatever they could to help me. "Thank you. I appreciate that more than words can say."

Mary reached across the coffee table and squeezed my hand. "We're family, Sean. And family is always there for each other."

Amid the warmth of their comforting words and the quiet chatter of our children in the kitchen, I realized how important the bonds we shared with others truly were. Those connections gave us strength to carry on even when it seemed impossible.

2

DECLAN

Three and a Half Years Later

It wasn't every day I had the Secret Service in the car behind me. But ever since last month when my friend Fallon's dad had won the U.S. presidential election, Fallon had Secret Service agents shadowing him. Since we wanted to go to the nightclub Chrome, we had a car full of agents following us as Fallon drove us, including two of our friends, Marco and Luca. It was cool, to be honest.

"Why are you so quiet?" I asked Fallon. It wasn't like he was stressed about school; we were on winter break.

He glanced over at me and then back at the road. "Am I?"

"Um, yeah. Usually, you're talking our ears off."

He lifted a shoulder. "Just thinking."

"About what?"

"Trying to think of a way I can get laid with all these Secret Service agents around." He looked in the rearview mirror.

"Can't you go to someone's place and have the agents wait outside?" That hadn't been the case several weeks ago when I'd gone to his place a few days after the election. Fallon and I were good friends, but also fuck buddies, plain and simple. We normally hooked up on Friday nights after a long ass week at law school just to let off some steam, and to, well, get off. But that night, we had ended up not fooling around because an agent had been stationed inside Fallon's condo. We hadn't been together since, but I wondered if Fallon had worked out some sort of deal to scratch that itch. Or maybe if neither one of us found someone to hook up with at the nightclub, then he could work it out so we could fuck.

"Maybe. I haven't had the chance, but if I find someone tonight, I can talk to Agent Bernard."

"Can you imagine not getting laid for the next four years?" Marco chuckled in the back seat.

"Hell, no," Luca and I said at the same time. The thought made my dick want to cry.

"There has to be a way," I wondered. Since the Secret Service knew who I was, maybe they would give me and Fallon time to be alone. They could frisk me to make sure I had no weapons, and I wouldn't mind Agent Davis, who attended class with Fallon, running his hands up and down my entire body. Maybe we could talk him into a threesome.

Ten minutes later, Fallon pulled his Mustang up to the front of the club. We stayed inside the car while the agents went inside to do whatever it was they did to make sure things were safe. Once they gave us the all-clear, we stepped out. People looked at us like we were famous, so I winked and played the part, scanning the line for any cute guys I might want to talk to later. But there was no time to gawk as they ushered us inside, and we made a beeline for the bar.

We ordered our drinks, Fallon paid, and then we turned to watch the dance floor.

After several minutes, Luca asked me, "Anyone catching your eye?"

"Not yet."

"What about you, Fallon?" Luca turned to him.

"Nah. You?"

"There is one hottie out there." He pointed his finger toward someone on the dance floor. The guy was cute from what I could see in the dim lighting. He had dark brown hair and a nice-looking body, but he wasn't what I was looking for. I wanted to find someone a few years older who could maybe have their way with me, or at least show me a new move or something.

"Don't do it," Fallon told Luca. "That guy's bad news."

"Really? You know him?" he asked.

Fallon nodded. "We were in the same fraternity. We were friends until he tried to fuck over my friend Tyler. It was a whole thing, and I haven't talked to him since."

"That's a shame," Marco chimed in. "He's cute."

"He's too young for me," I stated. "I'm thinking I want to try someone older. Maybe have him teach me a few things."

"Oh, I wouldn't mind finding a daddy," Marco agreed.

"Well, I didn't say I wanted someone that old. Not sure I want shriveled balls in my mouth."

We all laughed, but then Fallon said, "I need to hit the little boys' room. I'll be back."

"Already breaking the seal?" I teased him.

"Fuck, I know." He chuckled. "Can't help it."

He downed his drink and placed the empty cup on the bar. Agent Bernard, who was the one with us at the bar while the others walked the room or stayed outside, followed as Fallon headed toward the restroom. A few minutes later, Fallon returned to our group with a slightly serious expression on his face. He leaned in and spoke to us in a low voice. "Guys, I hate to do this, but I need to leave."

"What? Already?" Luca protested.

"Yeah, there's something urgent I need to take care of. It's a family thing," he explained, glancing at Agent Bernard. "But you guys will find a ride home, right?"

"Of course," I said. "Is everything okay?"

"Yes. Just, you know, being the son of the next president of the United States."

"We were right. Fallon is going to be cock blocked for the next four years." Luca shook his head.

"Trust me," Fallon stated. "That will not happen, but catch you guys at school after break is over."

As Fallon and Agent Bernard made their way toward the exit, I turned back to my friends. "All right. Who's ready to dance?"

The three of us chugged our drinks and then got out on the dance floor. While we danced, my eyes roamed the crowd, and I spotted a guy who appeared a few years older than me sitting at one of the high-top tables a few feet away. He had light brown hair that was slicked back, bedroom eyes, and was clean-shaven. Intrigued, I danced over to him.

"Hey," I greeted with a smile. "Mind if I join you?"

He gave me a once-over before grinning. "Not at all. I was hoping someone would ask."

As I slid into the seat across from him, our eyes locked in a way that sent a shiver down my spine.

"So, what brings you out tonight?" I asked.

"Needed a break from reality," he confessed. "You?"

"Tonight's all about losing myself in the music and maybe finding a bit of trouble along the way." I grinned.

His lips curled into a smirk. "Trouble can be a good thing if you know how to handle it."

I leaned in a bit closer, our faces just inches apart. "Do you know how to handle it?"

His warm breath grazed my ear as he said, "Guess you'll have to find out."

"Then let's see what you've got." I held out my hand and he took it. Guiding him a few feet to the dance floor, we began to move with the rhythm, our bodies swaying in sync. The heat between us was palpable, the tension building with every passing second. We hadn't told each other our names and I was totally cool with that because I really didn't need to know his name when all I wanted to do was fuck him.

After a few songs, he said into my ear, "My place isn't too far from here. Wanna join me?"

I smirked. "Lead the way, stranger."

3

DECLAN

A Year and a Half Later – Present Day

Walking into Ashford, Nolan & Torrance, I couldn't help but feel a surge of excitement because I could see my career goals within reach.

I had spent the previous summer between my second and third year of law school interning at the criminal defense firm and was looking forward to working as a law clerk and then a junior associate once I passed the bar in a few months. I really loved working for ANT, and my boss, Sean Ashford, was one sexy man for someone twice my age. Having him to admire each day was an added perk.

Navigating through the maze of cubicles, I exchanged greetings with familiar faces. Camille, the paralegal I'd become friendly with when I was an intern, greeted me with a smile.

"Hey, Camille! Long time no see," I called out.

"Hey, Declan! It's good to see you again. Are you back for good?"

"Hope so." I beamed and leaned against the entry of her cubicle. "Anything new to report since I left?"

It had been almost nine months since my last day, and I knew a lot could change in that amount of time. Plus, some sort of gossip was always going around and I was here for it.

She chuckled. "Oh, Declan, you have no idea what you've missed. This place puts the most outrageous lawyer dramas on TV to shame."

I raised an eyebrow, intrigued. "Spill the tea, girl."

She leaned in conspiratorially, her voice dropping to a hushed tone. "Remember Amy from billing? Well, rumor has it she's been having secret rendezvous with the new hotshot from investigations. And get this, they've been using the storage room on the eighth floor as their hook up spot!"

I gasped, playing along with her scandalous tone. "No way! Amy, the quiet and shy one, and a new investigator? That's juicy."

She nodded, enjoying the gossip session. "But wait, there's more. Remember Emily, Luke's new paralegal who everyone had a thing for last summer?"

Everyone but me because I didn't bat for that team. "Yeah, what about her?"

She grinned, reveling in the sizzling details. "Well, word on the office grapevine is that she and Luke have been spotted leaving fancy restaurants together, and others swear they saw them holding hands in the elevator."

My jaw dropped because Luke Nolan was a partner. "Luke Nolan and Emily? That's unexpected. I thought he was married."

Camille's eyes widened as she nodded with a huge smirk on her face. "He is."

"Nooooo," I breathed.

"But you didn't hear any of that from me." She winked.

I shook my head in disbelief. "This place is crazier than I remember. I thought I was coming back to a normal law firm."

She laughed. "Normal is overrated, Declan. Welcome to the real-life legal drama. Buckle up; it's going to be a wild ride."

I said goodbye to Camille before we both got into trouble. Not wanting to leave out the man who had hired me and the one I looked up to, I reached the corner office and knocked lightly on the open door.

"Good morning, boss. Great to see you again," I announced, my voice filled with genuine warmth.

Sean Ashford, the silver fox himself, looked up from his computer and returned my smile. "Declan Rivers! Welcome back. How've you been?"

He stood, and we shook hands. I had to force myself to let go because fuck, my boss was hot. He was quite a package, with his hair I wanted to run my hands through, piercing dark eyes that made me weak in the knees, and a smile that lit up a room. Looking at him made my dick twitch. Too bad he was straight or I would have been interested in starting my own office rumor.

"Doing good. Glad to be done with law school."

"I bet. Are you ready for the bar?" He sat back in his high-back leather chair.

"Getting there. To be honest, I'm nervous as hell."

"You'll do great." He waved off my concern. "And if there's anything I can help with, you just let me know."

"Of course. Thank you."

"Glad to have you back. I have a feeling this place is going to be a lot livelier with you around. Now, let's get you settled in."

OVER THE NEXT FEW DAYS, I SETTLED INTO THE FAMILIAR RHYTHM OF work life at Ashford, Nolan & Torrance. The thrill of being surrounded by brilliant minds and the constant buzz of activity fueled my determination to show I was worthy of a promotion once I passed the bar. As I split my time between studying for the upcoming bar exam and diving into the details of ongoing cases, I couldn't wait for the day when I would be the lead attorney on a case.

One morning, as I sifted through a stack of case files at my desk, Camille approached with a sly grin. "Declan, Sean wants you to assist on the Whitman case. He asked that you get the case file and head to his office."

My heart skipped a beat. The Whitman case was a high-profile embezzlement matter with its fair share of complexities. This was my opportunity to prove myself beyond the confines of intern duties. I gathered the files, headed to Sean's office, and knocked on the door.

"Come on in, Declan," he called, and I stepped inside.

"Morning, boss. I heard you need an extra pair of hands on the Whitman case," I said, presenting the files with a confident smile.

He nodded, motioning for me to take a seat. "That's right. It's going to be a challenging one, but I believe you're up to the task."

"I am," I assured him.

"Then let's get to work."

4

Sean

"Let's call it a night," I said, swiping my hand down my face. It was after midnight, and I was exhausted from the long day of reviewing reports from the forensic accountants and trying to create a theory of defense for the Whitman case. "I'll see you two bright and early on Monday morning."

Camille packed up and quickly rushed out of the conference room, leaving me and Declan behind. I was surprised he wasn't in a hurry to leave. Most guys his age would be eager to get their weekend started.

"So, how was your first week as an official employee of Ashford, Nolan & Torrance?" I asked as I closed my laptop and put it into my bag.

"It's been great. Thanks again for the opportunity to work here."

"No need to thank me. You impressed the entire firm last summer. The other partners and I wanted to offer you a job once you graduated. We didn't hesitate when you applied."

He smiled, his brown eyes brightening. "Wow, that means a lot, Mr. Ashford."

I chuckled. "You know you can call me Sean. Everyone else in the office does."

We walked out of the conference room together. "All right, Sean. So, do you have any big plans for the weekend?"

The entire floor had cleared out; the only sound in the office was the low hum from overhead lights. "My kids are coming over for dinner tonight, but other than that, I'll probably spend some time here going through more of those accounting reports. What about you?"

"Fallon and I are getting together to study for the bar tonight, but that's it, as far as plans go."

"See if you can convince him to give criminal law a try," I teased.

I'd known Fallon his entire life, and from a young age, he'd talked about becoming a lawyer. His father and I had hoped he'd follow in our footsteps, but he'd gone a different route toward becoming a civil rights attorney. It was an honorable career for sure, but it would have been nice to work with a Donnelley again.

Declan laughed. "Oh, I've tried. I thought it would be fun for us to work together, but you know him. He's set on changing the world."

"Yeah, he wasn't receptive when I mentioned it either."

We stopped at his cubicle, and he grabbed his bag and slung it over his shoulder. "Well, I hope you have a good weekend. Don't work too hard."

"You too." I grinned. "The bar is important, but you still need to find a little time for fun."

"I always do," he replied with a mischievous gleam in his eye and headed toward the elevator.

THE AROMA OF FRESHLY BAKED BREAD HIT ME THE MOMENT I WALKED in the door. It was almost seven, so Ryan and Morgan would be showing up any second. The three of us got together for dinner at least once a month, and on those nights, my personal chef, Jasper, would stay to serve our meal instead of simply preparing food for me to eat whenever I got home.

I knew my kids probably had better things to do than have dinner with me on a Friday night, but I was grateful they took time out of their busy, fun-filled schedules to hang out at the house. The truth was, the only time I wanted to be home was when they came over. The quiet got to me when I was alone, weighing me down like a suffocating blanket.

It had been five years since Melinda had passed away, and the void she'd left could still be felt. She had been the heart and soul of this house, filling it with happiness and love. Without her, everything seemed just a little bit colder. I'd considered selling the place and moving into an apartment closer to my office, but I worried about how Ryan and Morgan might feel about me selling their childhood home. It was filled with a lot of happy memories for them.

I climbed the stairs and dropped off my bag in my office before going to my room to change out of my suit. When I made my way back downstairs, I went to the kitchen to check on dinner. As I rounded the corner, Jasper greeted me with his usual smile as he put the final touches on our meal.

"Good evening, Sean. Dinner should be ready in about ten minutes."

"Thank you," I replied, peeking in the oven. "It smells amazing, as always."

Jasper nodded appreciatively. "I've prepared your favorite, sir. A roasted chicken with rosemary and thyme, garlic mashed potatoes, and steamed vegetables."

"And your famous rolls?" I asked with a grin.

Jasper was an incredible chef. Everything he made was excellent, but those buttery rolls were my weakness.

He chuckled. "Of course."

A couple of minutes later, I heard the front door open.

"Hey, Dad!" Morgan called out.

I turned around to see my daughter walk in. She was dressed in a floral sundress, and her light brown hair was piled high in a bun that looked haphazard but probably took her a long time to do. Morgan was a social media influencer, so her appearance was always carefully crafted and photo-ready. I didn't fully understand everything that went into her job, but I was grateful she'd found something that made her happy, and I would always support whatever she wanted to do.

"Hi, sweetheart," I said and wrapped her in a big hug. "How's it going?"

She squeezed me tight and then pulled away. "Things are good. Been busy."

We walked to the dining room and took our usual seats. "Yeah? How's your fashion channel going?"

Her eyes lit up with excitement. "I hit a million followers last night, and I've been offered some amazing sponsorships lately. Plus, I have some exciting collaborations lined up for the next few months."

"That sounds great," I said, proud of her accomplishments. "You've worked hard to build your brand, and it's paying off."

Just then, Ryan walked in. "Damn, it smells good in here. I'm starving."

"Hello to you too," I chastised playfully.

"Hi, Dad." He leaned down and wrapped an arm around my shoulders before sitting beside me. "Hey, sis. What have you been up to?"

Morgan smiled at her brother. "Oh, you know, the usual. Traveling, attending events, taking pictures."

"Living off Dad," Ryan added.

Morgan glared at him. "He paid for your apartment at one point too."

"Yeah, when I was in college. You're twenty-five and he's still paying for your place."

"Whatever," she huffed.

"I'm just saying, you probably make enough money from your videos that you could afford to support yourself."

"Just because you're a financial advisor doesn't mean you know everything. Besides, if Dad doesn't have a problem with it, you shouldn't either." She looked at me. "Right?"

"Don't bring me into it. I can't believe you two still argue like little kids." I chuckled.

Before they could continue with their childish antics, Jasper entered the dining room carrying a platter of roasted chicken and placed it on the table.

"Dinner is served," he announced.

"This looks great, Jasper," Morgan said, shaking out her napkin and placing it on her lap.

"I'm sure it tastes as good as it looks," Ryan said, winking at Jasper.

"Hopefully," Jasper replied with a smile. "Enjoy."

Once he was out of earshot, Ryan turned to Morgan and said, "Damn, he's hot."

I nudged his foot with mine under the table. "Don't talk about our chef like that."

"Why not? It's true."

I rolled my eyes. I couldn't have him starting something with someone who worked for me because if it ended, someone could get hurt. And if it was Jasper who was the one to get hurt, that could cause problems since I was his employer.

"Because some lines shouldn't be crossed. Flirting with an employee is never a good idea."

He smiled but raised his hands in surrender. "Fine. I'll behave myself, but that doesn't mean I can't admire him from a distance."

I shook my head, trying to hide my amusement. "Just remember, he's off-limits."

Morgan giggled, her eyes sparkling mischievously. "What about you, Dad? Anyone caught your eye recently?"

I took a sip of my water before answering. The first time one of my kids brought up the possibility of me dating again, I was surprised. I figured they wouldn't want me to move on, but they explained I was too young—even at fifty—to spend the rest of my life alone. A part of me agreed with them, but I wasn't in a hurry to meet anyone new.

"No, sweetheart. Work keeps me busy enough. I don't even have time to think of dating."

The conversation shifted to lighter topics as we enjoyed our meal together. Morgan shared stories of her recent travels and fashion collaborations, while Ryan gave us investment advice. I tried to give them my full attention, but my mind drifted in another direction. Maybe it *was* time for me to think about dating again.

5

DECLAN

I groaned as I rolled over and shut off my alarm. The night before I'd left the office after midnight. Now I had to get up and spend my Saturday with Fallon at his condo to study for the bar exam. I didn't mind the late nights at the office, but having to get up on a Saturday at nine was a real bitch.

Rubbing my eyes, I caught the smell of coffee lingering in the air, evidence my roommate Sam was already awake. I wasn't sure how she did it. She worked late hours as a bartender at a sports bar but somehow managed to get up before noon most days.

As I swung my legs over the edge of the bed, my gaze drifted around my small room. It was a far cry from the trailer park I grew up in back in Pennsylvania, where life was a constant struggle. My mom, a hardworking woman with three jobs, did her best to make ends meet. We lived paycheck to paycheck in that mobile home park. I knew she had it hard, and I tried my best to make it easier for her. I studied most nights, got good grades, worked part-time as a busser at one of the diners she worked at, and stayed out of trouble.

My efforts paid off when I earned a full-ride scholarship to the University of Pittsburgh. The relief on my mom's face when she heard the news was etched in my memory, but I hadn't stopped there. I aimed higher and received a scholarship to Hawkins Law in Boston. She no longer had three jobs, but I was still determined to make enough money to get my mom out of the rundown trailer community and into something better. Something nicer. Something bigger.

Dressed in only pajama pants, I sauntered into the kitchen to be greeted by the sight of Sam sitting at the table, sipping her coffee. She looked up, a knowing smile on her face.

"Rough night?"

"The attorney I'm working under doesn't like to leave the office until the cleaning crew arrives. I want to prove myself so I stay and help him as much as I can." Plus, he was so fucking hot for a silver fox. I didn't mind really.

"You're making your dreams come true, Declan. It's bound to be tough. But hey, at least you've got me to keep the coffee flowing."

"Yeah? You want to come be a private barista and bartender for Fallon and me today while we study for the bar?" I poured my coffee.

"I would if I didn't have to work this afternoon. Those secret agents look really hot in their suits and I wouldn't mind watching them all day."

"Yeah, they do," I agreed with a knowing smile as I added creamer to my coffee.

When Fallon first got his security detail, I wondered what it would be like to have Agent Rhett Davis put his hands all over me. Little did I know he was putting his hands all over Fallon in the same way I'd wanted. It was cool. Fallon and Rhett were now engaged and getting married in a couple of months. What started as a forbidden love affair would soon become their forever. As for me? I wasn't sure when or if I'd ever find someone. I was more of a one-night stand kinda guy, at least since Fallon and I stopped fucking around. I'd actually never had a serious relationship. I wasn't opposed to them. I had just been focused on my education. Now, I was studying for the bar and working for a promotion to junior associate. Once I met those goals, maybe then I would look for something a little more serious.

Taking a seat at the small table, the conversation turned to Fallon and Rhett's pending nuptials.

"Speaking of Fallon and his hot agent. How are they doing with wedding planning?"

"As far as I know, good. Fallon's mom is doing most of it."

Sam stood to make herself another cup of coffee. "Those guys are lucky to have found each other. It's like a real-life romance novel."

"Yeah," I agreed, my thoughts drifting to my own uncertain romantic future. "I wonder when—or if—I'll find someone like that."

She leaned against the kitchen counter. "It's okay to put yourself out there and let things fall into place, you know?"

I nodded. "You're right. I just need to figure out the right balance between chasing my dreams and, well, having a life."

She raised an eyebrow. "Who said you can't have both? Maybe the perfect someone will stroll into your life when you least expect it."

"Here's hoping." I raised my coffee cup in a mock toast.

She raised her mug and mimicked the motion against mine. "You will."

STEPPING OFF THE ELEVATOR, I NOTICED A SECRET SERVICE AGENT where he stood down the hallway outside Fallon's door. I wasn't sure who he was, but he was tall, had a chiseled jaw and, I would bet, strong biceps under his black suit. The one I'd seen walking the perimeter of the building wasn't bad either.

The agent at the door nodded in greeting as I approached, and then I knocked on Fallon's door. It swung open a few seconds later.

"Hey, man! Come in." Fallon grinned.

I stepped into the lavish condo, and he shut the door behind us. "Thanks. How are you?"

"Good. Ready to take this fucking bar exam already. What about you?"

"As ready as I'll ever be." I set my bag on his couch. "But working on a case with Sean Ashford has added a whole new level of pressure for me."

"You're the one who wanted to work for him." Fallon chuckled as he headed for the kitchen, and I followed.

"Can you blame me?" I smirked, picturing his salt and pepper hair, smoldering brown eyes, and strong jaw.

"Don't you say it."

"What?" I grinned.

"We aren't talking about how hot my uncle is."

Sean wasn't Fallon's uncle by blood, but a long-time family friend. That didn't stop Fallon from acting horrified anytime I mentioned that I found Sean attractive. "But you admit he's hot?"

"Dude." He opened the fridge and pulled out two bottles of water. He tossed me one. "I don't look at him that way."

"But I do." I waggled my eyebrows. We walked back to the living room, and I asked, "Where's Rhett?"

He had to be in the condo somewhere because I hadn't spotted any other agents inside Fallon's place. That only happened when Rhett was home.

"He's in the bedroom, I think."

Just then, Rhett walked into the room, looking hot in a hoodie and jeans that hugged his perfect ass. *Yeah, yeah. It was wrong for me to check out my friend's man. Sue me.*

"Hey, Declan. Ready to use all that legal brainpower?" he asked.

"Always. And speaking of power, I have to say, your Secret Service buddies are looking quite ... formidable today," I remarked with a sly grin.

Rhett rolled his eyes and shook his head in amusement. "You know they're here for a reason. It's not all fun and games."

Fallon laughed. "Lighten up, Handsome. Declan's just appreciating the view."

Rhett snorted a slight laugh. "All right, I'll leave you two to your studies. I've got to pick up Poppy for ballet. Don't get into trouble while I'm gone."

As Rhett left, I couldn't resist teasing my friend. "It's like your man knows you or something."

"Trust me. He knows every inch of me." Fallon winked.

I could have joked I did too, but instead, we settled onto his couch and got to work studying as another agent came inside and *protected* us.

THE CLOCK ON THE WALL SEEMED TO TICK LOUDER AS THE NIGHT WORE on, and I could feel the weight of the embezzlement case bearing down on my tired shoulders. As a law clerk on the cusp of becoming a junior associate, working late had become the norm, especially with Sean guiding me through the details of how to prepare for the upcoming trial.

"Let's order some food. We'll need the energy to get through these financial records," Sean suggested, glancing at the mountain of paperwork on the conference room table.

"Good. I'm starving," Camille groaned.

I chuckled and pulled out my phone, scrolling through the options for takeout.

"We can do Chinese, pizza, burgers from The Backyard ...?"

"We did those last week," Camille whined slightly.

"I should have my personal chef bring us dinner on these late nights," Sean suggested.

"You have a personal chef?" I asked.

Of course, he had a chef. Sean Ashford spent too much time in the office to have time to cook.

"I do. My wife used to do the cooking but ..."

He trailed off, looking down at the legal pad in front of him. I didn't know much about his personal life other than he was best friends with Fallon's parents and therefore dubbed Uncle Sean. He'd had a wife, but she died a few years back. I didn't know the details of her passing.

"What does he cook?" Camille wondered aloud, breaking the awkward silence.

"Everything." Sean smiled. "I'll chat with him tomorrow, but for now, let's order something we haven't gotten recently."

I continued scrolling through the options on my phone. We settled on a local Mediterranean place that none of us had tried before and was still open. As I placed the order, my stomach growled, a subtle reminder that we were working late into the night.

Just as the order was confirmed, Camille's phone rang, and her expression turned serious after she answered the call. I could see the concern in her eyes as she listened intently to the voice on the other end.

"I'm sorry. I hate to bail, but I've got to go," Camille said as she hung up. "My son is sick, and I need to be there."

Sean nodded. "Of course, Camille. Family comes first. Take care of what you need to, and we'll manage here."

Camille quickly gathered her things, apologizing for the abrupt departure. We assured her it was no problem, urging her to take care of her child. After she left, I could sense by how quiet it was that Sean and I were the only ones left in the entire office.

"All right, it looks like it's just you and me now. Let's tackle these financial records before that food arrives." Sean shifted his focus back to the task at hand.

We delved into the paperwork as the clock continued its relentless ticking. I tried to keep my attention on the work, but every so often, I would glance at my boss, admiring how sexy he was for someone old enough to be my father, and then I would continue with my work.

Once the food arrived, the smell of Mediterranean cuisine filled the room and we dug into the savory food.

Sean looked up from his to-go box, meeting my gaze with a small smile. "Good choice. This is a nice change from the usual takeout. We should explore more local places."

"Absolutely. I'm always up for trying something new."

As we continued eating, the conversation flowed naturally between work and more casual topics. He shared stories from his early years as a lawyer, and I found myself hanging onto his every word. His charisma and confidence were captivating, and it was easy to see why he had become the stellar attorney that he was.

During our conversation, his dark eyes locked with mine, and a subtle smirk played on his lips. "You know, I appreciate how hard you've been working on this case. You're doing an amazing job."

I felt a warmth spread through me at the compliment, and I couldn't help but reciprocate. "I've learned from the best. Your guidance has been invaluable."

His gaze lingered for a moment longer, and then he chuckled, breaking the intensity. "Flattery will get you everywhere, Mr. Rivers."

I blushed, realizing that perhaps my admiration had been a bit too obvious. "I just speak the truth, Bossman."

He cleared his throat and grabbed a stack of bank records. "All right. Where were we?"

6

Sean

"Come on, Morgan," I mumbled as I circled my daughter's apartment building.

The moment I drove past the lobby doors, a text message from her popped up on my phone:

> On my way downstairs

I searched the street again for a parking spot but didn't find one. Frustrated, I drove around the building once more and then double parked near where she stood waiting. I hopped out quickly and heaved her suitcase into the frunk of my silver Porsche 911 while she got into the passenger seat. Her shit barely fit.

"We're only going to the Cape for the weekend. How much did you pack?" I asked, climbing back into my vehicle.

Morgan rolled her eyes. "Faye and I are going to hit up a couple of parties while I'm there, and I haven't decided what to wear yet. It all fit, right?"

As I merged onto the road, she grabbed her phone and began typing away. For the past three years, the thing seemed to be glued to her hand.

"Yes, it all fit. Are the parties for business or pleasure?" I wondered.

She smiled brightly. "Both. One of them is sponsored by a company that just reached out to me about promoting their new line of sunglasses. The other is a private event that Faye snagged an invitation to. Rumor has it, Surrender is going to be there."

I glanced at her briefly. "Jasper's brother's band?"

"Yep."

"And they're just hanging out on Cape Cod?"

Morgan shrugged. "I don't know, but the lead singer is gorgeous, so I'm not missing that party."

"I'm surprised you've never asked Jasper to introduce you."

"I would have, but they all moved to L.A. This is the first time they've been back on the East Coast in a couple of years. There are rumors they're going to announce a tour soon. I'll make sure to ask Jasper if he can hook me up with tickets for that."

"Well, it sounds like you're going to have a fun weekend," I said, even though my partying days were long behind me.

"Speaking of fun." She twisted in her seat to face me. "My friend Madison told me her mom's divorce from husband number four is final. She thought we should set you guys up on a date."

"What?" I scoffed. "You want to set me up on a date? And with someone who just got divorced for the *fourth* time?"

I'd been out of the dating game so long—more than twenty-five years—I wasn't sure if I was brave enough to jump back in. Especially with someone who recently broke up with their partner.

"It's just one date," Morgan said, as though it wasn't a big deal. "You haven't gone out with anyone since ..." Her voice trailed off.

Since her mother died.

"It would be a casual thing," she continued. "Madison's mom is sweet and really pretty for her age."

"Wow." I chuckled. "But even with that ringing endorsement, I don't need my daughter playing matchmaker for me."

She crossed her arms. "Well, someone has to since you seem to have given up on finding love again."

I sighed, keeping my eyes focused on the road. "It's not that I've given up, Morgan. It's just ... hard."

She reached over and gently squeezed my hand. "I know it's been tough since Mom's been gone, but she'd want you to be happy."

I couldn't help but feel she was right and thought maybe I had let my grief consume me for too long.

"Okay," I finally said, glancing at my daughter with a small smile. "I'll think about dating, but you aren't setting me up with someone."

"Fine. Maybe you should try a dating app," she suggested.

I shook my head. "Absolutely not."

"Why? There are some great ones out there. I just created a profile on The Click—"

"That's why." I barked out a laugh. "I'm not going to be on the same dating app as my kid."

"Yeah, that's a good point," she agreed. "Just promise me you won't sit at the house all alone when you're not working. Promise me you'll get back out there."

"I promise." I glanced over my shoulder and switched lanes. "But speaking of the house ... I wanted to talk to you and your brother about me possibly putting it on the market."

My plan had been to wait to talk to Ryan and Morgan together, but Ryan rarely went with us to the Donnelleys' house. Not only was he extremely busy with his job, but as all the kids got older and started doing their own things, only Morgan and Faye remained super close.

"You want to sell the house?" The hint of sadness in her voice was clear.

"I'm thinking about it. I don't need that much space anymore, and living closer to work sounds nice. But I won't do it unless you and your brother are on board with the idea."

Morgan took a moment, her gaze fixed on the passing scenery. "I actually think that's a great idea. It can be part of your new beginning.

And if it means being closer to work and having more time for yourself, then why not?"

Her response surprised me a bit, but I was grateful for her understanding. I only hoped Ryan felt the same way.

As we continued our journey toward Cape Cod, Morgan's phone buzzed with notifications, undoubtedly messages from her friends, and updates on the upcoming parties. I couldn't help but feel a pang of nostalgia as I watched her get lost in her digital world. It seemed like just yesterday she was a young girl, riding in the back seat of my old Lexus GX, excitedly telling me about her day at school. Our entire lives had changed since then, but as she liked to remind me, my life wasn't over, so I needed to get out there and enjoy it.

An hour later we pulled into the circle driveway of the Donnelleys' two-story summer home on Cape Cod. The gray house stood tall, with its large windows reflecting the bright afternoon sun. At the front, a porch with a row of rocking chairs invited guests to sit and enjoy their beautiful yard, where the scent of saltwater mingled with the sweet fragrance of blooming flowers.

When I stepped out of the car, memories flooded back like a tidal wave crashing against the shore. The Cape Cod home held so many cherished moments for my family: the laughter of children playing near the water, the scent of barbecues and fresh seafood filling the air, and the warmth of friendship. Actually, Patrick and Mary Donnelley were more than just friends; they were family to me. We didn't spend as much time together since Patrick had been elected president of the United States, but we tried to get together whenever they could sneak away to the Cape.

Morgan climbed the steps in front of me, passing several Secret Service agents along the way. When Faye swung the front door open, they ran into each other's arms as though they didn't see each other in Boston all the time.

"Come up to my room. I need help picking out an outfit for tonight," Faye said.

"Dad, can you bring in my bag when you get yours?" Morgan asked but didn't wait for a response as Faye dragged her up the stairs.

"Some things never change, do they?" Patrick pulled me in for a quick hug.

I chuckled. "Apparently not."

Mary walked over and also embraced me. "Do you want a drink?"

"After the week I had, I think I need one."

"What's going on?" Patrick poured each of us a glass of Macallan on the rocks.

Our bags could wait, but a drink with the president couldn't.

"Just the usual: too many cases, not enough hours." I took a sip of the whisky he handed me, relishing the smooth burn that washed away the stress of the week.

"I remember those days." Patrick led us to the living room adorned with nautical decor.

While their house hadn't changed much over the past few years, it definitely had a different vibe now that Patrick was the president. Still, I'd been around the agents enough that eventually they blurred into the background and things didn't feel awkward.

Mary placed a meat and cheese tray on the coffee table and sat beside her husband on the couch. While reminiscing about the years Patrick and I worked together, we heard a car pull up.

"The boys must be here," Mary announced, a grin spreading across her face.

A minute later, Patrick and Mary's son, Fallon, and his fiancé, Rhett, walked in. Once hugs and greetings had been exchanged, they sat as well.

"Glad you guys could make it." Patrick took a drink of his whisky.

Fallon smiled. "Me too. It feels like forever since we've come to the Cape."

Rhett nodded in agreement. "Yeah, it's nice to take a break from the city and enjoy some fresh air."

"How's my little princess doing?" Mary asked.

Rhett's face lit up at the mention of his daughter. "She's good. Unfortunately, her mother had already planned to visit her parents. Otherwise, we would have brought her with us."

It still seemed strange that the little boy I once knew was now old enough to marry a man with a child. And from what Patrick and Mary had told me, it sounded like Fallon was a natural with her. That didn't surprise me. Whenever Fallon set his mind on something, he put all his energy into it. I was sure being a stepparent would be the same for him.

I turned to Fallon. "So, how's the job going?"

He grabbed a piece of cheese and a cracker from the charcuterie board before answering, "So far, so good. I'm learning a lot, and I think the Brighton Law Group is a really good fit for me."

I nodded. "Well, they're lucky to have you."

Before he could respond, his phone rang. "Hey, Declan. What's up?" he greeted, standing to move to the other side of the room.

My ears perked up at the mention of my employee. I tried to listen in, but Patrick pulled me back into conversation.

"So, what else has been going on with you?" he asked.

"Nothing much to be honest. I spend most of my time at the office."

Mary tilted her head in concern. "You're not working too hard, are you?"

"You both know how it is."

Patrick nodded. "Yeah, but you need some balance in your life."

"Okay, Mr. President. I'm sure you've figured out how to balance it all."

"Touché." He chuckled.

"You're not the only one who's said that though." I took a sip of my whisky. "On the drive here, Morgan mentioned wanting to set me up with the mother of one of her friends."

"Are you going to go?" he asked.

I shook my head. "I'm not opposed to dating, but I don't want my daughter setting me up. I'd rather just meet someone and let things progress naturally."

Mary's eyes flicked to something behind me and she asked, "Is everything okay?"

I glanced over my shoulder to see she was talking to Fallon.

"Yeah, I invited Declan up here for the weekend. Don't worry, I informed the Secret Service ahead of time." He turned to his father and winked before sitting back in his seat. "We've been studying for the bar together and figured a change of scenery might help us out a bit. Anyway, he ran into some car trouble, but he's on his way now."

"So everything's good?" I inquired, and Patrick and Mary both glanced at me. "He interned at the firm last summer and started as a law clerk a couple of weeks ago," I offered as an explanation for why I was suddenly concerned about their son's friend.

"I hope that's okay with you," Fallon said. "I didn't think having your employee here would be a problem."

"Not a problem at all."

Why would it be?

7

DECLAN

Betsy was on her last leg. She was my twenty-something-year-old Kia Sportage I'd had since I'd turned eighteen seven years ago. We'd been through a lot together. From my first blow job, to me moving to Boston and having to make the five-hour drive with her loaded down with everything I'd owned at the time, which hadn't been much more than my clothes.

Of course, as I drove to Fallon's parents' Cape Cod home, she overheated. It wasn't unusual, especially in the summer, but it still sucked. I had to pull over, wait for it to cool down and then I topped her off with antifreeze. I kept water and antifreeze in the trunk for that reason because I never knew when she would have a meltdown.

As I pulled up to the house, the Secret Service guys gave me a quick nod and then I parked behind a silver Porsche I'd never seen before. It wasn't my first time at the Donnelleys' Cape Cod home, and I didn't think the car belonged to anyone in the family unless Faye had gotten a new one. I knew their brother Finnegan wouldn't be at the house because ever since his actions had almost gotten Fallon killed, he hadn't been invited to things that involved Fallon.

Grabbing my bag out of the back, I walked up the stairs and the door swung open. Fallon welcomed me with a huge smile.

"Welcome," he said and stepped back so I could enter. "We're just having a drink and catching up. Do you want anything?"

"Sure. Whatever everyone else …"—I trailed off as I saw Sean sitting in a seat next to Fallon's dad—"is having."

Our eyes locked, and we both smiled.

"Mr. Rivers." Sean greeted me and stood to shake my hand. I realized the Porsche must be his, even though I'd never actually seen what he drove before.

"Bossman. Didn't know you'd be here." We shook.

"You can never say no to the president." He chuckled.

I walked to Mr. Donnelley and stuck out my hand. "Mr. President."

He stood. "How many times do I have to remind you that you can call me Patrick?"

"I know, but it's not every day I get to rub elbows with the leader of our country. My friends back home would be jealous."

We shook too. "I'm not the president here. Just think of me as Fallon's father."

I knew he was trying to put me at ease, but it was hard to think of him as anything but the president, since Secret Service agents were everywhere and he *was* the president of the United States, but I went with it.

"Of course." I smiled and hugged Fallon's mom.

I turned and grabbed the drink Fallon had poured for me. It looked like whisky, but I didn't ask. Instead, I shook Rhett's hand. "Good to see you, man."

"You too," he replied.

"What's this about car trouble?" Sean asked.

My eyes flicked to Fallon, and he lifted a shoulder.

"Betsy loses her cool sometimes," I stated.

Everyone stared at me as though I had two heads.

"My car. Sorry. I named her Betsy," I explained as I took a seat next to Fallon and Rhett on one couch.

"You named your car Betsy?" Rhett questioned.

I took a quick sip of the amber liquid, and it was definitely whisky. I felt it burn all the way down my throat. "Yeah. Didn't think Bertha fit. She's not that big."

The room erupted into laughter.

"I think Betsy is a fine name for a car," Patrick said.

"Don't tell her that. She'll want me to buy her new tires or something," I joked, as though my car would gloat over the compliment and demand a gift.

"Does she break down often?" Sean asked.

I took another drink of the liquor. "Only on long drives. I can usually get to and from the office without a problem."

"Good." He bobbed his head up and down. "Don't want you to get broken down on the way to work, or worse, stranded at work."

"There's always a stranger's car," I deadpanned.

Sean stared at me and then Fallon clarified by saying, "He means a rideshare."

"Oh." Sean chuckled. "Right."

"It sounds to me like your boss needs to pay you more." Fallon grinned at his uncle.

"He'll get a promotion and a raise once he passes the bar," Sean stated.

I smiled at my boss, appreciating his consideration. I just needed actually to pass.

"Speaking of passing the bar, we should probably study a little bit since that's why you came." Fallon stood, and I followed suit.

"We'll call you boys when dinner is ready," Fallon's mom said.

Fallon kissed Rhett, and then led me to what I assumed to be his father's office. We studied until we were called for dinner and then we joined everyone in the backyard. Fallon's sister, Faye and another woman, Morgan, who I learned was Sean's daughter, also joined us. I knew Sean was best friends with the Donnelleys, but I had no clue he had a daughter the same age as me.

After dinner, Faye and Morgan left for some party and the rest of us sat around the fire pit as the sun went down and talked amongst ourselves. Everyone slowly called it a night and went to bed until it was just me and Sean left. Neither one of us made a move to go to bed; instead we stayed next to the fire and enjoyed the heat. I wasn't going to leave him alone, so I took the opportunity to talk to him one-on-one.

"It's so peaceful out here," Sean stated as he leaned his head against the back of the Adirondack chair and looked up at the dark twinkling sky.

"It is," I agreed.

"Did you grow up in Boston?"

I shook my head. "No. Pennsylvania."

"Oh, really? Did you attend college there or Hawkins University?"

"Out there. Made the move when I got a scholarship for Hawkins Law."

"Oh wow. You must have done really well on your undergraduate GPA and LSATs."

"I did," I confirmed. I wasn't one to gloat, but I had busted my ass to make something of myself so I could help my mom and live a better life.

"I knew you were smart. Glad to have you on my team."

"I still have to pass the bar," I teased.

Sean chuckled. "Yeah, but I have no doubt you will."

"Hope so or it'll be even longer until I get my mom out of her trailer park."

Learning I had been raised in a trailer park and my mother still lived in one seemed to evoke no response from him. His lack of reaction surprised me, but then I wondered why it should. After all, I had no idea what his background was; I only knew him as the successful attorney with the Porsche. Maybe he came from nothing too.

"Are you planning on her staying in Pennsylvania or moving to be closer to you?"

"Ideally, I would love for her to be here and not have a job where she's on her feet all day, but I don't want her moving in with me, either. I'd like to make enough money to buy a house with an in-law suite or something. But not just a room in the same part of the house. Maybe above the garage so we can still have our space."

"That's very noble of you."

"Thanks. I want to help her out in any way I can."

"Is that why you went to law school? To be able to have a good income and help her?"

"Yeah. It was either that or become a doctor, but I'm too squeamish when it comes to blood."

"Good thing you weren't there when Fallon got shot then."

"Oh man. I still can't even believe that happened."

"I know. And I can't imagine what Patrick and Mary went through. As a father, your heart aches for your kids when they get hurt and to hear one of them was shot—I just can't."

"Is Morgan your only child?"

"No." He shook his head. "I have a son two years older than her."

"Oh, that's right. I've seen a picture in your office, but they were much younger."

"Yeah, and now everyone is gone."

I glanced over at him. "Gone?"

"I mean, it's just me living in the house now."

"Oh ... right. How long has it been since your wife passed?" I had no idea why I was asking him. I felt like a jerk bringing up his dead wife, but I was curious. I wanted to know everything there was to know about Sean Ashford.

"It's been a little over five years."

"I'm sorry," I breathed.

"Fuck cancer, right?"

"Absolutely. It's what killed my father too."

"Damn, Declan. I didn't know." He reached over and squeezed my arm. His hand lingered just slightly before he pulled back.

"It's okay. I barely remember him. He died when I was six and it's just been me and my mom ever since."

"She never remarried?"

"No." I shook my head. "She worked three jobs while I was growing up, and even now, she works one as a waitress at a diner and takes extra shifts when she can so she can keep paying her bills. Not sure she has time to meet anyone."

"Morgan wants me to date again," Sean admitted.

"Is that not what you want?"

"I don't know. It would be nice to have someone I could go out to dinner with, or go to movies with, but no one will ever replace my wife."

"You know, you don't have to twist my arm. I'll go to dinner and a movie with you." I wasn't sure if it was time for my jokes or not, but how could I skip the opportunity to tell Sean I would date him and pass it off as a joke?

Sean threw his head back and laughed. "But I'm your boss."

"Meh. You're only my boss at the office."

8

SEAN

It was a typical Monday morning at Ashford, Nolan & Torrance. It wasn't even nine yet, but the office was bustling with activity. Colleagues exchanged pleasantries with me as I left the break room with a cup of coffee in hand and headed to my office.

"Good morning, Sean," Camille greeted me when I reached her desk. "Did you have a good weekend?"

"Good morning," I returned. "I did. It's amazing what a couple of days on the Cape can do for a guy."

She smiled. "Well, hopefully, you got some rest because your calendar is full this week."

"Noted." I took a sip of the coffee. "I'll meet you and Declan in the conference room shortly."

"Sounds good." She smiled and got back to work while I entered my corner office.

Once I settled into my chair, I opened my laptop and went straight for my inbox. A ton of emails had accumulated over the weekend, and I searched for the ones I needed to reply to immediately. After I responded to the most urgent ones, I gathered my files and headed toward one of our large conference rooms.

Declan and Camille were already inside, going over documents from the Whitman case.

Declan's head popped up when I stepped through the doorway, and he grinned. "Hey, Bossman. How's it going?"

"Morning, Declan. Just another manic Monday." I chuckled, thinking of the song he likely was too young to know. "What have you and Camille been up to?"

Camille glanced up from her notes and flashed a smile. "We were just reviewing the witness statements. Two of them have conflicting stories, so we need to see what's going on there."

I nodded and took a seat across from Declan. "Okay, add that to the list. For now, I want us to finish with the bank records."

As the morning progressed, we probably downed a gallon of coffee as we discussed the best way to present our defense of Christopher Whitman. Declan's passion for this career path was evident when he offered ideas for me to consider. It made me think of the conversation we had shared Saturday night while we sat around the fire at the Donnelleys' house.

I would never have guessed he'd faced so much hardship growing up. I had felt a sort of connection with him when he'd mentioned his father had died of cancer when he was a young child. I knew how hard Melinda's death had been on our children, and they had been adults at the time; I could only imagine how scary and traumatizing it was for a six-year-old who likely didn't understand what was happening.

A couple of hours later, the conference room phone rang, and I answered it. "Hey, Lauren. What's up?"

"District Attorney Zimmer is on the line for you. Would you like me to transfer the call to the conference room or your office," she replied.

"I'll take it in my office. Just give me a moment before sending him through."

"Of course."

I hung up and stood. "Why don't you two take your lunch while I deal with the DA's office."

Camille pushed her chair back. "After all that caffeine, I need water more than food."

"Do either of you want me to grab you a sandwich from the deli across the street?" Declan asked.

"That'd be great. I'll take a pastrami and Swiss on rye with Russian dressing." I pulled a couple of twenties from my wallet and handed them to him. "It's on me since you're picking it up."

Declan pocketed the money and said, "Thanks. I'll head over now."

We all left the conference room and turned in different directions. Walking into my office, I closed the door and answered the call when Lauren transferred it to me.

"Zimmer, it's good to hear from you. What kind of deal do you have for my client?"

He gave me the offer and we talked it over. After we hung up, I called my client and went over the specifics of what had been proposed. We had already discussed the likely scenarios and his best options, so the call didn't take long.

Declan was alone when I returned to the conference room, eating his sandwich while flipping through a file.

"Thanks for this." I sat and began unwrapping the sandwich he had placed in front of my seat, along with my change.

"You're welcome. Although I should thank you since you paid."

"Nah, you fly, I buy." I took a bite, and once I swallowed, I asked, "Where's Camille?"

He shrugged. "She needed to make a call. She said she wouldn't be long."

"All right. We'll fill her in on anything important when she comes back."

We got back to work, and I reached for a manila folder. As I grabbed it, my finger slid along the edge, and I felt the sharp sting of a paper cut.

"Shit," I muttered.

Declan swung his gaze my way. "What's wrong?"

"Just a little paper cut." I searched for another napkin, but the only one I had was the one my sandwich was lying on.

He rummaged through the bag from the deli, pulled out a clean one, and walked it over to me. "Here you go."

I moved to take it from him, but when he looked down at my injured finger, he gasped. "Uh, that's a lot of blood for a paper cut."

"It's a little bigger since it was from a folder. I'll be fine." I wrapped the napkin around my finger.

When I looked up, Declan looked slightly pale, and I remembered his words from our talk two nights ago.

"It was either that or become a doctor, but I'm too squeamish when it comes to blood."

"Are you okay?" I asked.

He nodded. "Yeah. Like I said, I'm not a big fan of blood."

"Well, lucky for you, I'm not bleeding out over here. It's just a tiny cut," I responded, hoping to make it seem as though it wasn't a big deal.

Declan swayed on his feet. Beads of sweat formed on his forehead, and it appeared as though all the color had drained from his face.

He tried to speak, but his words came out as a whisper. "I ... I don't feel so good."

Without hesitation, I stood and guided him back to his chair, urging him to sit down before he collapsed.

"Lean forward and take a few deep breaths," I directed, crouching in front of him and placing a hand on his shoulder. "Just focus on your breathing."

He followed my instructions, his breaths becoming steadier with each deep inhale and exhale. All the while, I rubbed his shoulder in an effort to comfort him.

Once his breathing evened out, I grabbed his water bottle and handed it to him. "Here, have some water."

He took it with a shaky hand and lifted it to his lips.

After a few moments, he sat up straighter in his chair.

"Thanks," he said, staring into my eyes. "That was embarrassing."

I shook my head and stood. "There's no need to be embarrassed. At least you'd told me about your blood aversion, so I didn't worry something was really wrong."

"Who knew you'd get a front-row seat to one of my freak-outs?" he teased as he started to relax.

"I'm just glad I didn't have to pick you up off the ground. Not sure these old muscles could handle that." I laughed.

He looked me up and down and smirked. "Somehow, I doubt that."

I chuckled while internally flattered by his compliment. At least, I thought it was a compliment. Declan often said things that were hard to decipher. Sometimes, it just sounded like friendly banter and other times, I detected a hint of flirtation in his words. As someone who took pride in being able to read people, I was intrigued by the fact I couldn't quite figure him out.

Before I could respond to his comment, the door swung open, and Camille walked in. Her eyes widened when she caught sight of Declan's pale complexion. "What happened? Is everything okay?"

"Just got a little dizzy for a minute, but I'm fine now, thanks to my hero over there." He pointed at me as I returned to my seat and threw a wink in my direction when Camille turned toward me.

Maybe he was flirting.

9

DECLAN

The last two days were hell.

I knew the bar exam was going to be intense, but I was mentally exhausted, having finished almost five hours of testing on day one, and the 200-question exam and the ten essay questions the next day.

Fallon was still taking the exam, so I left the room, grabbed my bag from the storage area, and sent him a text:

> Text me when you're done and let's meet for a drink

I walked over to the Secret Service agent who was waiting for Fallon. "I'm going to head over to Flanagan's if Fallon wants to meet for a drink. Just sent him a text."

"Yes, sir," the agent replied. I thought his name was Vance.

I walked the few blocks to the sports bar where I knew my roommate, Sam, was working. She spotted me right away and waved me over to an empty seat at the bar.

"Well?"

"I don't know, but I'm glad it's over."

"I know you did amazing. What can I get you to drink? It's on me."

I thought for a moment. "Peach Long Island."

"Ohhh it was that bad?"

"Just need to forget about it. Nothing I can do now."

"All right. At least I know you're not driving."

No. Betsy was at home, and I'd gotten a ride with Fallon and his escorts. If Fallon went directly home to his man, I'd take a rideshare back to my apartment when I was ready.

Sam placed my drink in front of me. "Can I get you something to eat?"

"Yeah. I'll take the fish and chips."

"Coming right up."

Taking a sip of my cocktail, I made a face as the alcohol slid down my throat. "Damn, Sammy. Trying to kill me?"

She glanced over and grinned from where she was punching my order into her kiosk. "You're the one who wanted mostly alcohol in your drink."

"You're right. Just wasn't expecting it." I could have sworn my stomach was already warming from the one sip.

"Don't get soft on me now, Rivers," she teased.

I chuckled. "Honey, I'm never soft."

I took another swallow of the potent Long Island, feeling the stress of the bar exam slowly fading away, and my phone buzzed in my pocket with a text.

> Fallon: On my way

As I stuck my phone back into my pocket, Sam slid a plate of fish and chips in front of me.

"On the house. You deserve it after surviving that torture of an exam."

"You're the best." I stuck a fry into my mouth.

Sam dealt with her customers while I ate my food and waited for

Fallon. Several minutes later, the door swung open, and two of Fallon's Secret Service agents walked in.

"Now this just made my day," Sam gushed as she stared at the agents. Maybe Fallon needed to hook her up with one.

I chuckled and with everyone else in the bar, I watched as the men did their sweep and then walked out. A second later, Fallon came inside. He joined us at the bar, and Sam immediately greeted him.

"Fallon! Congrats on completing the bar exam."

He smiled. "Thanks, Sam. How'd you think you did?" he asked me.

I lifted a shoulder. "Not sure. You?"

"I feel good, but who knows."

"Exactly. I think I did well, but we won't know until we get the results in October."

"What can I get you to drink, Fallon?" Sam asked.

"What are you drinking?" he pointed at my half-drunk cocktail.

"Peach Long Island."

"That sounds about right. I'll have what he's having and the fish and chips as well."

"Eating too?" I questioned. "You don't need to go home to Rhett?"

"He's having dinner with Poppy at her favorite restaurant and then taking her to her mom's. I have a few hours."

"I'm sure he'll help you *unwind* later." I waggled my eyebrows.

The memory of what Fallon and I used to do every Friday night to *unwind* after a week of classes flashed in my head.

"I'm sure he will." Fallon smirked.

"But speaking of hot agents. Think we can hook Sammy up with Agent Vance or one of the others?"

My roommate's blue eyes widened. "Declan!"

"You have the hots for Vance?" Fallon grinned.

I stuck another fry into my mouth. "She has the hots for all of them."

"I do not." She swatted me playfully with a bar towel.

"Don't lie to the man. You're always talking about his agents." I winked at her. She was probably going to poison my coffee in the morning.

"He's single," Fallon confirmed.

"There you go," I stated.

"And what about you?" she questioned. "You're single too."

"And gay," I reminded her. "I'm only pining after one straight man, honey."

"Oh, god," Fallon groaned.

"Who's that?" Sam asked.

I glanced at Fallon and then back at my roommate. "My boss, Sean."

Sam's eyes widened. "Seriously? You didn't tell me that!"

"There's nothing to tell. Like I said, he's straight, but he's so hot."

"Stop," Fallon protested and covered his ears.

"You stop." I playfully slapped his arm. "You're acting like I'm talking about your dad."

"He is like a father to me."

"But he's not. He's not even blood-related to you."

Sam leaned against the bar, a mischievous twinkle in her eyes. "Well, if you're looking for a distraction, I could always set you up with someone. I'm sure someone here is looking to get laid."

I chuckled, taking another sip of my drink. "Let's see how the night goes."

Sam shrugged and pointed at my drink. "Fair enough. Another?"

"Yes, ma'am."

As Fallon and I ate our fish and chips and drank our drinks, we talked about what we thought the toughest questions on the exam were. Once I had a good buzz going, Fallon's phone dinged with a message. He checked it and smiled.

"Rhett just finished dinner. I should head home."

I nodded. "Go on. Enjoy your night and I'll see you at your bachelor party."

"Can't wait." We shared a bro hug.

Fallon paid his tab, said goodbye to Sam, and left the bar with his agents in tow.

Sam immediately came to me and leaned on the bar again. "Well, now that Fallon's gone, are you going to spill the tea on this boss crush of yours?"

Damn, that bit of gossip had to have come out at least forty-five minutes ago. My girl must have been dying the entire time.

I chuckled, shaking my head. "No details to spill. It's just a silly crush because, like I said, he's straight."

"There's no hint that he may be bi?"

I thought about all the times I'd been alone with Sean. In some of those moments, it seemed like he may have flirted back when I had flirted, but he was probably only being nice. If he was flirting it wasn't obvious.

"Doubt it."

"Another drink?"

I scanned the bar and didn't see anyone my type. "Actually, I'm going to head home and change, then hit up Chrome. See you in the morning?"

"Be safe," she warned, pointing her finger at me.

"I will, Mom. But if there's a sock on the door, don't come inside."

"Oh no." She shook her head. "You take that to your bedroom."

"Nah. I'll just go to his place."

"All right. See you in the morning and I'll have a big cup of coffee waiting for you."

"As I said before, you're the best."

It had been a busy week at work, and I was leaving the office later than I had planned. I drove past the address Tyler Statler had sent me for Fallon's bachelor party. On the front of the brick building, huge, neon pink letters announced "The Illusion Lounge," and I instantly recognized it as the home of one of Boston's most well-known drag shows.

When discussing how to celebrate Fallon's upcoming nuptials, he asked for something fun but low-key. I wasn't sure how a drag show would fit that request, but I couldn't wait to find out.

I pulled into a parking garage a couple of blocks away and found a space. Once I parked and locked up Betsy, I started the short walk to the lounge.

Heading inside, I saw Agents Vance and Shea standing near the table where Fallon and Tyler were sitting with Fallon's sister Faye and Sean's daughter Morgan. I let out a small sigh because I didn't particularly care for Faye. While Fallon was down-to-earth and laid-back, Faye was the opposite and came across as elitist and conceited. I hadn't interacted with her or Morgan much during the weekend on Cape Cod, but I was also under the impression they felt as though they were too good to be associated with me. For whatever reason, there had been a few eye rolls and the look of disgust on their faces over that short weekend. It didn't bother me because I wasn't looking to be friends with them.

Still, this was my friend's bachelor party, and if he wanted his sister to be a part of it, who was I to complain?

"What's up, party people?" I called out over the music playing as I approached the group.

"Declan!" Fallon stood and hugged me.

"Sorry for running late."

"No worries. We're still waiting for Marco and Luca."

"Yeah." Tyler stood and shook my hand. "Hopefully, they'll get here in time for dinner."

I lifted an eyebrow. "Dinner?"

He nodded. "They do a dinner show here, and after, we're going to the nightclub downstairs to meet up with Rhett and his friends."

"That's cool," I replied as I took a seat between Fallon and his sister. "Hi Faye, Morgan," I greeted.

"Hello, Declan," Faye responded coolly.

Morgan said nothing, but it was possible she hadn't heard me because of the music.

Soon, our server came over to take my drink order. I scanned the drink menu and chose a sherry blossom cocktail made with strawberry vodka and champagne.

As the server walked away, Faye and Morgan excused themselves to go to the restroom, leaving Fallon, Tyler, and me to chat.

"How's married life?" I asked Tyler.

"It's good, we actually just got selected by a birth mom to adopt her baby."

"Holy shit," Fallon and I said at the same time.

"Yeah. She's not due until the spring so we have some time, but it's still scary."

"That's amazing," I stated. "Congrats."

"Thanks." Tyler beamed.

Fallon stood and hugged Tyler. "Yeah, congrats. Parent life is fun when they don't throw tantrums over having to eat something other than snacks."

"Can't wait to come to you for parenting advice." Tyler slapped Fallon's back as they hugged.

"Me either, and when she's old enough, Poppy will be your babysitter." The two guys pulled apart and Fallon's gaze landed behind me.

"Hey, guys!" he said.

I turned, expecting to see Marco and Luca walking in, but I didn't expect to see the two of them holding hands.

"So, we have some news," Luca stated and held up their connecting hands before sitting across from me.

"Wait!" I looked at all my friends, wondering if they were pranking me. "When? How? I have so many questions."

"Well, while you and Fallon were busy this summer studying for the bar exam, the two of us often hung out alone," Marco explained.

"And one night, after a few drinks, one thing led to another, and ... well, I'm sure you can figure out the rest," Luca added.

"Did you know about this?" I asked Fallon.

"No. I'm as surprised as you are."

I chuckled. "It's definitely a shock, but I'm happy for you guys."

The server returned with my drink, and I took a sip. "So, let's see, Tyler is married and going to be a dad, Fallon's about to be married and become a stepdad, and now you two are dating. That leaves me as the only single one here?"

I wasn't sure whether I was relieved not to be tied down or disappointed they all had somebody and I didn't.

"You're going to stay that way too, if you keep lusting after straight guys." Fallon barked out a laugh.

Luca placed his elbows on the table and leaned forward. "Sounds like there's a story there."

I rolled my eyes. "No story. I just have a tiny crush on my boss. That's all."

"His boss, who also happens to be a close friend of my family and is twice Declan's age," Fallon stated.

"Oh! You found yourself a daddy, did you?" Luca grinned.

Fallon made a gagging sound. "I'm going to kick all your asses for putting that image in my head. Uncle Sean—"

I smacked my friend's arm. "Be quiet. His daughter is coming back."

Thankfully, our server returned as soon as Faye and Morgan sat down.

"Are you all ready to order?" the server asked.

"You guys go first," Luca suggested. "We still need a second to look at the menu."

The Illusion Lounge offered a wide selection of Asian dishes, and I chose the sesame soba noodles and another sherry blossom.

Shortly after we got our food, the house lights dimmed, and a spotlight illuminated a figure in a black sequin dress standing on stage.

"Good evening, everyone! Welcome to The Illusion Lounge. My name is Ophelia Cox, and I'll be your hostess tonight. Now I know what you all are thinking. 'Ophelia, you're so gorgeous.'" She gave a twirl, and we all cheered. "'How can the other queens even compete with you?' To answer your question, they can't, but be nice to them, anyway. They're trying their best."

Everyone laughed, and she began making her way into the crowd. "A little birdie told me we have a special guest tonight." She stopped next to our table. "Supposedly, a certain politician's son is marrying his Secret Service agent, and he's here celebrating his last few moments of freedom." Her eyes flicked over to where Vance and Shea stood. "Hell, honey, if all the agents look like those two, I can't blame you for snatching one for yourself. I'd let them guard my body any day."

It was hard to see, but I was pretty sure Vance was blushing.

"Anyway, we have a great show for you, so gird your loins because you're in for a wild ride." "Vroom Vroom" by Charli XCX started playing. "Our first performer is my drag daughter. She's young, she's fun, and she may or may not be hung. Give it up for Enlarga Cox."

We watched in awe as Enlarga lip-synced while flipping and dancing across the stage. Toward the end of her performance, she weaved through the tables, collecting tips along the way, and I was glad I had some small bills in my wallet.

"Let's give it up for my daughter. Just like her mother, she'll do anything for a dollar."

The show continued with some more dancers and a couple of comedy routines. Ophelia returned onstage as the show wrapped up and addressed the crowd. "As they say, all good things must come to an end. Thank you for spending your night—and hard-earned cash—with us. In a world where some don't want to see us shine, we appreciate you supporting your local queens. Goodnight, and keep sparkling like the true stars you are."

The crowd erupted in applause and then started to disperse. After we settled the bill, our group went downstairs to the nightclub. The music was pumping, and I couldn't wait to get out on the dance floor.

"Is Rhett here yet?" Fallon asked Vance as he looked around the dimly lit space.

"Not yet, but Day just texted that they're on their way."

Day was also an agent and Rhett's close friend who would be acting as his best man at the wedding. They had done their own thing tonight, but knowing how head over heels Fallon was, I knew he was happy they'd end the night together.

"Okay. Let's grab a table while we wait," Fallon suggested.

"I'm going to get another drink," I announced. "Do you guys want anything?"

Fallon nodded. "I'll take a Sam Adams."

"I'll have the same," Tyler added.

"Got it." I turned to Faye and Morgan. "How about you two?" I would have asked Marco and Luca, but they had disappeared somewhere, and I could only guess what they were up to.

Morgan was the first to answer. "We'll go with you. We need to look at the cocktail menu before ordering."

I shrugged, surprised how she didn't roll her eyes and complain that I was talking to her. "Cool."

The three of us sauntered over to the bar, and the bartender came over immediately.

"What can I get you tonight?" he asked.

"I'll take a Stella and two Sam Adams. Also, whatever these two would like." I gestured to Faye and Morgan.

It took a few seconds before they finally settled on a mojito for Faye and an appletini for Morgan.

A few minutes later, the bartender placed the five drinks in front of us and gave me the total. I pulled out my credit card and handed it over.

While he ran it through the card reader, I turned and looked out over the crowd, searching to see if anyone caught my interest. Unfortunately, none of them were as hot as the one guy I couldn't have.

Fuck, Fallon was right. I needed to stop lusting after Sean Ashford, or I might stay single forever. Not that I was necessarily looking to date. But this infatuation with my boss seemed to be holding me back from approaching other guys.

"Excuse me, sir," the bartender said, interrupting my inner musings, and I spun around. "Your card has been declined."

I balked. "Are you sure?"

"Yes, I ran it twice to make sure."

"Seriously, Declan." Faye laughed as she reached inside her purse.

I'd be damned if I was going to let her pay, though. I opened my wallet, grabbed my last sixty dollars, and handed them over.

While that had been embarrassing, I would not let it ruin my night. I was there to have a good time with my friends, and that was exactly what I was going to do.

10

Sean

With one last look in the mirror, I straightened my tie before grabbing my suit jacket and heading for the lobby. Ryan, Morgan, and I were staying at a beachfront resort the Donnelleys had booked for the guests while on the Cape for Fallon and Rhett's nuptials. Normally, I stayed with Patrick and Mary whenever I was in town, but with all the staff and wedding guests around, it was easier and more peaceful to stay at the hotel.

As I turned the corner, I saw my kids seated at the bar. Ryan had a bottle of beer in front of him while Morgan sipped an appletini.

"Looking good, Dad," Morgan sang when she spotted me.

"I would hope so. You picked out my suit." I smirked.

"You want something to drink before we go?" Ryan asked.

I shook my head. "I'm going to hold off until the reception. Patrick said he has a bottle of Macallan waiting for us."

"Whisky is so gross." Morgan scrunched her nose.

"That just means there's more for me." I grinned.

Ryan downed his beer, and while signing his tab, asked, "We're riding over in one of the shuttle buses, right?"

The Donnelleys had secured several buses to transport the guests to and from their house where the wedding was being held. According to Patrick and Mary, the Secret Service had made the recommendation to help alleviate some of the security concerns of so many people descending on their property.

"Yeah. I think those are the only vehicles they're allowing near the house," I explained.

"Well, let's get a move on. Faye texted that some hotties are there already," Morgan urged.

We walked through the large doors and approached the first all-black bus with tinted windows. Next to the door, a Secret Service agent holding a clipboard stopped us.

"Can I see your ID, please?" Each of us handed over our driver's licenses, and he compared them to what I assumed was a list of authorized guests. He handed us back our cards. "Great. Just need to search you and your bags." He looked through Morgan's small clutch and then ran a metal detector over both Ryan and I before giving us the okay.

The three of us boarded the bus, and after more people got on, the driver closed the door and began the ten-minute drive to the Donnelley estate.

Once we arrived, we stepped off the bus and made our way toward the backyard. A large white tent had been set up in the middle of the expansive property, and inside, chandeliers hung from the ceiling, casting a romantic glow over the tables covered with candles and floral arrangements. Beyond the tent were several rows of white chairs facing the small cliff, where a white archway framed the ocean view.

We took a seat in the row behind the chairs reserved for Fallon's family and waited for the ceremony to start. The sound of waves crashing against the shore filled the air while everyone got settled.

A few minutes later, a harpist began playing, and a little girl, who I recognized as Rhett's daughter, Poppy, started down the aisle. She wore a sapphire dress and sprinkled white rose petals along the way to the altar. Rhett, who wore a gray tuxedo with a bow tie that matched the color of his daughter's dress, followed her. His parents escorted him, and he joined his best man, already standing at the front.

A moment later, Fallon headed down the aisle, flanked by Patrick and Mary. He was dressed the same as his soon-to-be-husband and wore a huge smile on his face.

Once Fallon joined Rhett, they stood facing each other and held hands. The way they looked at each other, as though the other was their entire world, I couldn't help but believe they would enjoy a very happy life together.

"Friends and family," the officiant began. "Today we have the honor of witnessing Rhett Davis and Fallon Donnelley transform their love story into a lifelong commitment. To start the ceremony, Fallon's sister Faye will read a poem for the couple."

Faye, in a dress the same color as Poppy's, stood at the front and read "The One." When she finished, she returned to her seat and the officiant addressed Rhett and Fallon.

"Rhett, in the presence of everyone here today, do you take Fallon to be your lawfully wedded husband, to love, honor, and comfort him in sickness and in health for as long as you both shall live?"

Rhett flashed Fallon a bright smile and said, "I do."

The officiant asked Fallon the same question and I heard Mary sniffle as Fallon replied, "I do."

"And now it's time for the vows that Rhett and Fallon have written themselves."

Rhett cleared his throat and began. "Fallon, when I met you, I had a feeling I was in for an adventure. But never in my wildest dreams did I think it would include falling in love with you. Not only did you capture my heart, but you also welcomed Poppy into your life. Every day with you is filled with love and laughter, and I wake up excited for whatever comes our way. I promise to love you, to always be there for you, and to make our home a place filled with happiness. Here's to us, to our family, and to every moment yet to come."

Fallon spoke next. "When I first saw you, I thought you were hot." The crowd burst into laughter and Fallon grinned. "The day you were assigned to protect me, I figured I'd have a little fun driving you crazy, but it didn't take long for me to realize you were the person I didn't even know I was looking for. Every minute I spend with you makes me fall in love with you a little more. And when we have Poppy with us, I can't imagine life any better than that. Today, I vow to be the best partner possible to you, to share in your joys and your challenges, and to create a life for us filled with love and continued adventures."

I couldn't help but get a little emotional listening to them put their feelings into words. Finding someone you wanted to spend the rest of your life with was a gift that not everyone was lucky enough to experience. I'd had that kind of love once and I still missed her every single day.

After they exchanged rings, the officiant announced they could kiss. Rhett cupped Fallon's face in both hands and laid one on him while everyone in attendance cheered loudly.

The newlyweds walked hand in hand back down the aisle, both beaming with happiness. Then, the wedding planner announced that hors d'oeuvres and drinks would be served while the couple and their families were taking pictures, and the crowd began to move toward the tent.

I checked the seating assignments and noticed I would be sitting with Luke Nolan and his wife, along with a couple of Patrick and Mary's other friends. Ryan and Morgan would be at the table with Faye.

If I were going to make it through sharing a meal with Luke and DeAnna, the most unhappy married couple I knew, I would need a drink. I headed toward the bar and ordered a glass of whisky.

As the bartender poured my drink, I noticed someone step up next to me, and I smiled when I saw who it was.

"Hey, Bossman," Declan said, returning my smile.

"Declan," I greeted with a nod. "Nice ceremony, wasn't it?"

"Yeah. Not gonna lie, I teared up a little."

The bartender placed my drink in front of me and Declan requested a beer. After popping the cap off the bottle of Stella Artois, the bartender passed it over to him.

"The vows got me too," I admitted.

"Yeah, but that backdrop was amazing and perfect."

"It was," I agreed. "I also think Mary's been planning this wedding since Fallon and his siblings were babies. She just didn't know which one would be first."

"Yeah, I think some of us were surprised Fallon was the first to walk down the aisle."

I sipped my whisky, savoring the warmth as it slid down my throat. "Why's that?"

Declan shrugged. "It wasn't too long ago he was playing the field. But I have to admit, he's never looked happier. He and Rhett are a perfect match."

"What about you?"

He choked on the sip he took. "What do you mean?"

"Do you play the field?"

I had no idea why I asked him that question. It wasn't something I would typically ask an employee, but since the night we had talked around the fire, I've wanted to get to know him better.

"Pretty much." He smirked.

"So, no wedding for you?"

"Doubtful. It would take a pretty damn special guy to get me to settle down."

That was the first time I'd heard Declan mention he was gay, and it made me believe I hadn't been totally off base when I thought he might be flirting with me on occasion.

"Declan!" someone shouted, and we both turned around in time to see two guys who appeared to be Declan's age approaching us.

"Fallon and Rhett are ready for a celebratory shot," the taller one said while the other talked to the bartender.

The other guy glanced in my direction and looked me up and down, his eyes sparkling. "Who's this?"

Was he checking me out?

"Marco, this is my boss, Sean Ashford. Sean, this is my friend, Marco. And that one"—he pointed at the other—"is Luca."

"Oh, he's *the* boss," Luca said with a grin.

"Makes sense," Marco added.

What did that mean?

Declan shook his head and laughed. "Let's go find the grooms and do these shots. I'll catch you later, Sean."

"See ya," I replied.

I watched as Declan and his friends made their way through the sea of guests. With a slight shake of my head, I took another sip of whisky and decided it was time to brave my table where Luke and DeAnna were seated. As I weaved through the crowd, I caught sight of their strained expressions and instantly knew it was going to be an interesting dinner.

"Luke, DeAnna," I greeted them with a warm smile. "How are you enjoying the festivities?"

Luke's eyes flickered with a mix of surprise and relief at my arrival. He motioned for me to sit next to him while DeAnna continued staring off into the distance, her demeanor reeking of misery.

"The Donnelleys sure know how to put on a party," Luke stated, although his voice lacked any enthusiasm.

"That they do," I agreed.

Eventually, Fallon and Rhett were introduced and took their seats at the head table with Fallon's best man, Tyler Statler-Foster, and Rhett's best man, fellow Secret Service agent Collin Day.

Dinner was served, and the drinks continued to flow. Every once in a while, my eyes would find Declan at the table with his friends. They all seemed to be enjoying themselves, and it appeared they were well on their way to being drunk.

After the grooms shared their first dance and then did the mother and son dance, Mary came over to me with a beautiful woman at her side.

"Hi, Sean. Are you having a good time?"

I stood and hugged my friend. "I am. You did an amazing job with this wedding."

"Thank you." She beamed and then turned slightly toward the woman standing next to her. "Have you met my communications director, Jessica?"

"I don't believe I have." I offered my hand in greeting. "Nice to meet you."

Jessica reached out, and we shook. "It's nice to meet you too."

"Sean and Patrick started a law firm together twenty years ago and have been friends even longer," Mary explained. "Oh, would you look at that? It looks like the wedding planner needs something. You two should dance until I come back."

I glared playfully at my friend before she rushed off to the other side of the tent.

"Oh wow, this is embarrassing," Jessica muttered. "Mary's not getting any points for subtlety, is she?

"Probably not, but she means well." I laughed. "Besides, I like to dance."

"Me too," she replied.

I led Jessica to the dance floor, where we stayed for a few songs before the DJ announced that Rhett and Fallon would cut the cake. While everyone gathered around the couple, my phone buzzed in my pocket. When I pulled it out, I saw a text from Declan. My eyebrows knitted in confusion. We'd only texted about the Whitman case before, so why was he texting instead of coming over to talk to me? Swiping the screen, I opened the message.

> OMG Sam! This wedding is wild. Bossman is here and looking fucking delicious tonight *peach emoji* *eggplant emoji* *tongue emoji* Also some guy I hooked up with over a year ago is here. I've spent the entire reception avoiding him. FML

I had so many questions. Who was Sam? Who was the guy he hooked up with? And why was I a topic of conversation? Although I could admit I was somewhat flattered that someone thought I looked *delicious,* as he so eloquently put it, I didn't know how to handle the situation. Was I supposed to respond so he would know he sent the text to the wrong person? Or would it be better if I disregarded it altogether?

Ignoring it sounded like the better of the two options. With any luck, he wouldn't figure it out since he was probably drunk, and it would save us both a lot of embarrassment.

I shoved the phone back in my pocket and joined the crowd just in time to watch the happy couple feed each other a piece of wedding cake. Jessica and I danced some more, and then she rejoined some of the White House staffers as they called it a night.

Eventually, more guests began to leave, and I searched for Ryan and Morgan.

"Are you two ready to head back to the hotel?" I asked as I approached them at the table they were sitting at.

"I'm going to stay here with Faye," Morgan said.

Ryan was focused on his phone but still managed to say, "I'm ready whenever you are."

"All right. Let's go. I'll pick you up tomorrow, sweetie." I kissed my daughter's cheek.

"Night, Dad."

As Ryan and I made our way out of the reception tent, I stopped to say goodnight to Patrick and Mary.

"Are you guys leaving?" Patrick asked, wrapping an arm around my shoulders.

"Yeah, but we had a great time. Even if your wife tried to set me up." I smiled at Mary so she'd know I was teasing.

She gasped, clutching her chest as though she was offended. "I did no such thing. You guys live too far apart, anyway. I just wanted you to have some fun tonight."

"Well, mission accomplished." I kissed her on the cheek.

We said goodbye, and then Ryan and I headed toward the buses. When we reached the front of the house, I saw Declan and his friends stumble onto one of the buses. The door closed behind them, and we climbed aboard the other one.

Once back at the hotel, Ryan started for the elevator while I glanced toward Declan as he stood near the bar with his friends.

"Hey, you go on up. I'll see you in the morning."

Ryan turned to see where I was looking. "Who's that? He looks familiar."

"He's a friend of Fallon's and my new employee."

"Oh, okay. Are you going to go talk to him?"

I nodded. "Yeah. I'll see you at breakfast tomorrow."

"Sounds good."

Once the elevator doors closed behind my son, I walked over to Declan. "Hey, you doing okay?"

His eyes widened when he saw me. "Bossman! What are you doing here?"

The nickname had me thinking about the text he'd sent me by accident, and a small smile crossed my face as I thought about his compliment. "I'm just checking on you. Looks like you had a good time."

"I did, but now I want to go to bed."

"Don't be a party pooper, Dec," Marco whined.

"Yeah, we just ordered another round of shots." Luca tried to pass one to his friend.

Declan groaned but didn't respond.

"Why don't you guys hang out? I can make sure Declan gets to his room," I offered.

Marco lifted an eyebrow. "You sure?"

I nodded. "It's no problem."

Marco and Luca exchanged mischievous grins before shrugging and clinking their shot glasses together.

"What room are you in?" I asked as Declan and I waited for the elevator.

"316."

When we got into the elevator, he stood right next to me and leaned against the wall behind us.

"You smell good," he mumbled.

"Thanks," I replied, unsure what else to say.

A soft ding signaled our arrival on the third floor. As the doors slid open, I guided him toward his room. "Do you have your key?"

He reached into his pocket and pulled out the plastic card. "Yep."

It took him two tries, but he managed to open his door.

"Are you going to be okay?" I asked.

"Yeah, Bossman. I'll be good. Thanks for walking me up here."

"Okay." Our gazes met for a second. "Get some sleep, drink water, and take something for a headache before you fall asleep."

"Will do."

"See you on Monday," I said.

"See you on Monday," he replied and closed the door.

After tonight, Monday would be interesting for sure.

11

DECLAN

I WAS NEVER DRINKING AGAIN.

I was certain everyone had said those words at least once in their lifetime, but I meant them. Holy shit, did I drink too much at Fallon's wedding or what? I drank so much I didn't remember anything after dinner was served. But hey, I didn't puke, so that was a plus.

Luca had been the driver for the weekend because I didn't think Betsy would survive the trip. After he and Marco dropped me off at my building, I said my goodbyes to my friends and dragged myself up the flight of stairs to my second-floor apartment.

When I entered, Sam was on the couch with a big bowl of what looked like a salad on her lap.

"Oh god. Put that thing away," I groaned and shut the door.

"Put what away?" she questioned.

"Your food." I plopped down in the accent chair next to the couch.

She snorted a laugh. "Ah. You're hungover, my friend."

I closed my eyes and rested my head back against the chair. "So much that even if I smell alcohol again, I will barf."

"Nah. You'll be back drinking next weekend."

"Doubt it."

"There's half an avocado in the fridge I didn't use for my salad. It's yours. Make some avocado toast. It will help."

"Nothing will help." I needed to take something again for my throbbing head, but I was afraid even that wouldn't stay down.

"Trust me, it will, but tell me about the wedding. I take it you had fun?"

"Yeah, but I wish I could have sent you a pic of Sean and not just that text last night. I didn't get a picture of him."

"What text?"

I finally looked over at her. "The one I sent about how hot he looked."

"I never got a text." She reached for her phone and then said again, "Nope. Didn't get one."

I sat up, my head swirling with the sudden movement. "What do you mean, you didn't get one?"

"The last one I have from you is about bringing home dinner the other night."

I slipped my phone out of my pocket and went straight to my text messages. The room spun as I saw who I'd sent my last message to. "Fuck me. I'm really going to puke now."

"Why?"

I stood and paced. "I sent the text to Sean."

"No!" she gasped and covered her mouth with her hand.

I nodded, my stomach churning. "I need to quit my job now."

Sam set her bowl on the coffee table and then stood. She grabbed my arm to stop me from pacing. "You don't need to quit."

"Yes, I do. I'll never be able to look at him again."

She tried to suppress a smile, but her eyes betrayed her amusement. "Come on. It might not be as bad as you think. Maybe he didn't see it, or he's cool about it."

I scoffed, sinking back into the chair. "No, he saw it. There's no way he didn't. I even used emojis, for God's sake."

She laughed, unable to contain it any longer. "Well, emojis do add a certain level of commitment to the compliment, don't they?"

I shot her a glare. "This isn't a joke. He's my boss. My professional life is now a dumpster fire."

"Okay, okay," she said, attempting to compose herself and then returned to the couch. "Maybe he's the type to take it in stride. You know, stoked but unbothered."

"I hope so, but I should go draft my resignation letter now."

"Just go into the office, act normal, and see if he says anything. Maybe he didn't even read it. Maybe he was drunk too."

I sighed, considering her advice. "Yeah, maybe. But if he read it, I can't even imagine the awkwardness. I'll be the laughingstock of the office."

She grinned mischievously. "Or maybe he's flattered, and he'll ask you out. Romantic, right?"

I shot her another glare. "Your sense of humor is not helping. He's straight."

"Just trying to lighten the mood." She chuckled. "But seriously, don't jump to conclusions. You'll be fine. Now, eat that avocado toast and get some rest. Tomorrow is a new day, and who knows, maybe it'll all blow over."

I nodded, taking a deep breath. "Yeah, you're right."

"And for the record, there's no harm in appreciating a good-looking boss." She stuck a slice of cucumber into her mouth.

I managed a weak smile. "Easy for you to say when you're not the one who sent him an embarrassing text."

As I reluctantly headed to the kitchen to make that avocado toast, I couldn't shake the sinking feeling that Monday was going to be a day to remember.

THE NEXT MORNING, I WALKED INTO THE OFFICE WITH MY STOMACH IN knots, half-expecting an intervention banner and a choir singing a ballad about my drunken escapades. The office was surprisingly quiet, but as I turned the corner toward my cubicle, Sean was standing next to Camille's desk.

Trying to play it cool, I attempted a casual nod, but it came out more like a nervous twitch. His eyes met mine, and for a moment, an awkward pause lingered as we both didn't say anything.

"Morning, Declan," he finally greeted.

I mumbled a barely coherent response and hurried to my little alcove, desperately avoiding eye contact with anyone else. I set down my bag that had my resignation letter inside and then sat at my desk and woke my computer. My computer screen became the most interesting thing in the world as I fumbled with my keyboard, trying to appear engrossed in my work.

"Declan. Got a minute?"

My back stiffened and then I swallowed, not turning around to face Sean. "Sure thing."

I took a deep breath, mustered some courage, and decided to confront the awkwardness head-on. I followed him to his office, and we stepped inside. He walked to his desk and sat. I stood nervously just inside the door as I waited for him to speak.

"How are you feeling this morning?" he asked and leaned back in his chair.

Besides my heart hammering in my chest? "Good. Crazy wedding, huh?"

Sean grinned. "For some of us."

Oh, god. "Yeah. Did you have a good time?"

"Besides Mary trying to set me up with her communications director? It was nice."

My eyes widened and I took a step closer. "She tried to set you up?"

He nodded. "She did, but I just danced with Jessica for a while."

That I remembered. "That's it?"

He tilted his head slightly, and I finally sat, feeling a little bit more at ease, but not fully.

"Yeah, that's it. Why?"

I blinked and stammered out, "I ... I just thought maybe you ah ..."

"Took her home?"

I swallowed. "Yeah."

Sean chuckled. "Do you not remember me walking you to your hotel door?"

I stared at him for a few long seconds. "You helped me to my room?"

"You were pretty drunk."

Hello, God. Yeah, it's me. Can you just take me now? "Thank you. I don't remember much after dinner."

"Of course. So, how about we get to work?"

That was it? If he wasn't going to bring up the text, I wasn't either. "Sounds good."

As we discussed work matters, I couldn't help but wonder if he was intentionally avoiding any mention of my embarrassing text. Maybe he hadn't seen it after all, or perhaps he was just a master at brushing off awkward situations.

Over the course of the day, we exchanged the usual work-related banter, and I found myself gradually relaxing. Maybe, just maybe, the whole incident had been blown out of proportion in my hungover mind.

As the day unfolded, it became apparent that Sean was indeed taking the high road. He didn't make any snide comments or give me knowing looks. Instead, it seemed like he was determined to treat me the same way he always had, and the resignation letter in my bag was long forgotten.

THE OFFICE HAD EMPTIED, LEAVING ONLY SEAN AND ME TO WRAP UP the day's work. We exchanged a few last-minute comments about his pending cases as we gathered our belongings.

"Looks like once again we're the last ones standing," Sean commented with a half-smile.

"Yeah, seems like it," I replied, glancing around the deserted office. Even Camille had left.

As we made our way to the elevator, I couldn't help but feel a sense of relief that the day was finally over.

We stepped into the elevator, and as soon as it started to descend, a sudden jolt made my stomach drop. I exchanged a puzzled glance with Sean, and then the elevator just stopped.

"What the hell?" I muttered, pressing the button for the ground floor, however the elevator remained stubbornly still.

"Maybe it's just a glitch. Let's try the call button," Sean suggested, reaching for the intercom.

He pressed the button repeatedly, but there was no response.

"The timing couldn't be worse," I groaned. "Everyone is gone."

"Maybe not in the entire building. Someone has to be here still."

The lights flickered and then went out, plunging us into sudden darkness. A few seconds later the emergency lights overhead blinked to life, casting a dim glow that barely illuminated the small space.

"Great, just great," I muttered under my breath.

"Looks like we're having an impromptu team-building exercise. Bonding in the dark."

I couldn't help but laugh despite the situation. "Yeah, who needs trust falls when you have a malfunctioning elevator?"

"Let me call 911."

Could this day get any worse? Everything had gotten better, but now it was turning to shit again. How long did it take to get rescued from an elevator? What if we were trapped between floors? What if the cable broke and we dropped ten floors? Was this how I died? I was trying not to panic as Sean spoke to the dispatcher.

"Yes, the elevator stopped ... Probably between the eighth and ninth floor ... Myself and another employee ... No one answers." He pressed the call button again and still no one responded. "Nothing ... Really? ... Great ... Okay. Will do ... Thank you." He hung up. "It's going to be a while."

"Why?" I breathed.

"Warehouse fire or something."

"Okay, but what does that have to do with us?"

"All units are tending to the fire. They said they'll send someone as soon as they can." He loosened his tie and sat on the floor with his back against the far wall.

"As soon as they can? How long is that?"

"I don't know."

I slid down the wall next to him. "Well, this sucks."

"Not what you had planned for your Monday night?"

"Can't say it was. You?"

Sean shook his head. "I was going to have dinner with my son and research some condos for sale in the area."

"Buying a new place?"

"Would like to. My house is just too big for just me."

I understood what he meant, but I'd never lived somewhere that was "too big." Maybe one day.

"Fallon's building is nice," I remarked.

"Yeah, but not sure I want to live somewhere with Secret Service hanging around."

"Has to be super safe, right?"

"True."

I stared at the closed silver doors in front of us. I didn't want to take out my phone in case, for some horrible reason, I needed all the battery power I had left of it. Maybe it was because I felt the dim lighting was hiding me from embarrassment, but even though Sean didn't bring up my text, I finally had to get it off my chest.

"So about the text …"

"What text?"

My head snapped in his direction, and he was grinning at me.

"The text from Saturday night."

"Oh, *that* text." He chuckled.

Okay, so he was laughing. That was good. "Yeah, so … that wasn't meant for you."

"Obviously. Who's Sam?"

"My roommate."

"Did you tell him about it?"

I nodded. "I told *her*. Well, actually I also said …"

"Said what?" he prompted after I didn't say anything because I'd realized what I'd actually said to her when I'd thought I sent her the text.

"Nothing." I averted my gaze.

"Oh, come on. You have to tell me now."

I felt my cheeks heat. Lord, I had never been so embarrassed in all my life. I should have just kept my mouth shut and the text would have been long forgotten. "I ... uh ... said I wish I had taken your picture and sent that too."

He didn't say anything. Once I was brave enough, I peeked over at him to see he was staring at me. I could barely make out the smirk on his lips, but it was there. "Go on."

"What do you mean 'go on'?" I laughed nervously.

"Why'd you want my picture to send to her?"

Was he baiting me? "I actually meant so I could have a pic of you on my phone," I admitted.

Sean was still grinning. "Well, I'm flattered. Didn't know I was photo-worthy."

I rolled my eyes, trying to play off my embarrassment. "Please, I'm sure ladies bring you baked goods nightly."

His laughter was boisterous, and I had to join in because I liked watching him laugh.

"Bringing me baked goods? Are we in the 1950s?"

I lifted a shoulder. "I don't know. I don't date women."

"No, you just play the field, right?"

"Is that what I said?" Damn. I really needed to stop drinking.

"Something like that."

"I guess that's true, but I don't really date though."

"No?"

I shook my head. "Just a little nighttime fun sometimes."

"Damn, it's been a long time since I had some 'nightly fun'."

"All right, so the lady from the wedding is out, but didn't you say your daughter suggested you date again?" He nodded, and I continued. "So, go date."

He snorted a laugh. "I haven't dated since my twenties. I don't even know what to do."

"I don't think waiting for baked goods is the right way."

"I wouldn't turn them away, though."

We were laughing so hard about the entire situation that I had tears in my eyes. When we finally stopped, everything became quiet, and we stared at each other. My gaze dropped to his lips and then back up to his dark brown eyes. He did the same, and I ever so slightly moved my head closer to his. I could have sworn he leaned in as well, so I went even further. With only a few inches separating our lips, he didn't pull back. I ran my tongue along my bottom lip and, without any more hesitation, my lips met his.

The elevator jolted, and we scrambled to our feet as the lights came on and we started moving toward the ground again.

12

Sean

When the elevator doors opened, I rushed out and headed across the lobby.

Declan kept pace with me and said, "Sean, I'm sorry. I should never have done that."

I glanced around and confirmed we were still alone. "You don't need to apologize, but that can't happen again. I'm your boss."

He nodded. "Is that the only reason?"

I pushed open the door to the parking garage and walked toward my car in the first row. "What do you mean?"

"I just assumed the problem would be because I'm a guy."

Him being a guy hadn't crossed my mind when I considered the reasons why kissing Declan Rivers was a bad idea. I was more concerned about him being my employee and twenty-five years younger than me. But since he'd mentioned it, I was also starting to freak out a little about the guy part.

It wasn't as though I had a problem with the idea of being attracted to another man. I was open-minded enough to understand people's sexuality didn't fit into little boxes that some parts of society tried to force them into. That didn't change the fact I was in a situation I never expected and was struggling to wrap my head around everything.

I pressed the button on the door to unlock my car. "The reason doesn't matter because it was inappropriate. I shouldn't have let it happen, so that's on me. We can just forget about it."

"If that's what you want."

"It is. I'll see you tomorrow." I slid into the driver's seat.

"See ya," I heard Declan say before I closed my car door.

It took me a little over thirty minutes to drive from the office to my house in Weston, and I spent the entire time thinking of how Declan's lips felt against mine. It had only been for a few seconds, but I'd be lying if I said I didn't feel something when we kissed. And I wished it had lasted longer.

Was I into men but somehow never knew? I didn't think that was the case. While I hadn't dated much, it wasn't because I never found myself attracted to someone. I had noticed beautiful women plenty of times, but I'd never looked at a man the same way as I looked at women.

I was still trying to figure things out when I walked into my house. After setting my briefcase down on the console table in the entryway, I made my way toward the kitchen. Ryan's car was in the driveway, and it was likely I'd find him sitting at the island, flirting with Jasper, despite my warnings to leave our chef alone.

When I rounded the corner, my son was exactly where I thought he would be, his chin resting in his hand as he watched Jasper check something in the oven.

"Hey," I greeted. Both of them turned toward me. "Sorry I'm late. I hope I didn't ruin dinner."

Jasper shook his head. "It's fine. The lasagna and garlic bread are staying warm in the oven, and the salad is in the refrigerator. I'll make your plates now."

"Thanks," I replied and looked at Ryan. "I'm going to change really quick. I'll be right back."

"No problem, I don't mind hanging out with Jasper." Ryan smirked.

I chuckled and turned to leave, but not before I noticed the grin on Jasper's face.

After I changed into a T-shirt and joggers, I joined Ryan at the kitchen table while Jasper placed plates filled with steaming lasagna, Caesar salad, and rustic garlic bread, along with glasses of pinot noir in front of us.

"This looks great, Jasper. Thank you," I praised.

He smiled. "You're welcome. I hope you both enjoy it."

"I know I will." Ryan waggled his eyebrows, and I nudged him with my foot under the table.

Jasper laughed and then addressed me. "If you don't need anything else, I'm going to take off. There's a key lime pie for dessert in the fridge and your dinners for the rest of the week are in the freezer with heating instructions."

"Sounds great. I hope you have a good evening."

"You too."

As soon as he was gone, I gave Ryan a stern look. "I swear you're going to get me sued for sexual harassment if you keep that up."

He rolled his eyes. "Trust me, Jasper doesn't have a problem with me flirting."

Maybe he was right, but I couldn't stop myself from adding one more thing. I was a father, after all. "Just be careful."

"I will." He took a bite of the cheesy pasta and then asked, "Why were you late tonight? Still working on that embezzlement case?"

I took a sip of my wine. "I am, but that wasn't the reason. I actually got stuck in the elevator on my way out of the office."

"Seriously? That's wild. Were you by yourself?"

"No. One of my coworkers was with me." I didn't want to tell him it was the same guy I'd checked on at Fallon's wedding. While I had no reason to hide said coworker's identity, for some reason, I felt as if I uttered Declan's name, somehow my son would know what happened. I was fully aware of how ridiculous that sounded, yet I continued to keep the information to myself.

Our conversation shifted to the condo I was going to check out the next day, and all thoughts of Declan were forgotten ... at least temporarily.

WHEN I CLIMBED INTO BED LATER THAT NIGHT, THE MEMORY OF Declan kissing me in the elevator came rushing back. Over the course of the evening, some of the shock had worn off, and now I was left a little confused and oddly horny.

Without any hesitation, I kicked off my flannel pajama pants and pushed down my boxer briefs so I could wrap a hand around my hard shaft. I closed my eyes, and immediately, images of Declan sitting in the conference room, his sleeves rolled up to his elbows as he worked on a case, flashed through my mind.

After a couple of tentative strokes, the image changed to us back in the elevator and the way he looked at me with his intense brown eyes while licking his lips right before he pressed them to mine. Thinking back on it, I was pretty sure I leaned in before he kissed me, and I started to wonder what would have happened if the power hadn't come back on. Would we have stopped at only a kiss? Would he have wanted more? I could picture him cupping my dick as he invaded my mouth with his tongue, and I ran my palm over my tip then down my cock.

Reaching down further, I gently tugged on my balls with one hand and increased my speed with the other. My toes curled, and I knew I was getting close.

Switching up my rhythm, I gripped my dick with more pressure, and my hips began thrusting as I fucked my hand. I kept going, sweat forming on my brow, until I exploded all over my stomach and chest.

Once I cleaned up, I worried I would suddenly feel ashamed for jerking off to thoughts of my employee, but much to my surprise, all I felt was relief. It had been a while since I'd come that hard, and even though I'd told Declan we needed to forget about our kiss, I doubted it would be the last time I touched myself to thoughts of him.

13

DECLAN

Forget about it?

There was no chance in hell I would ever forget the kiss with Sean in the elevator.

Ever.

But I understood why he said what he did, in that moment before he slid into his car. He was my boss, and I was his employee, and a kiss between us was forbidden.

Or was it?

After getting into Betsy and making the drive back to my apartment, I tried to remember what the employee handbook said about interoffice relationships, and I couldn't recall if it indicated they were against company policy. If they were, then how was Luke Nolan hooking up with Emily, and Jonathan from investigations being with Amy from billing okay?

As I neared my place, a conversation I'd once had with Fallon ran through my mind ...

"You didn't tell me your uncle was hot as fuck." I'd said.

"He's my uncle, bro. I don't see him like that. Plus, he's straight."

'Plus, he's straight.'

Was he? If he were, he would have turned his head instead of leaning into the kiss, right? He would have pushed me away. He would have told me straight up he wasn't into guys. He would have done something other than let my lips taste his.

Pulling into my parking spot at my apartment complex, I cut the engine on Betsy and then grabbed my things and stepped out. After giving her a good girl pat on the hood for not breaking down on me, I headed upstairs. Sam was on the couch watching some reality show on Netflix, and I couldn't hide the grin that was still on my face from kissing Sean.

"Good day at work, I take it?" She paused the TV.

"Girl," I drew out the word and leaned against the closed door, letting my bag drop to the ground. "You have no idea."

"Your boss isn't upset over the text?"

I shook my head and pushed off the door. "No. We laughed about it."

"Well, that's good."

"Yeah, and then"—I couldn't stop grinning—"we kissed."

Sam's eyes widened, and she jolted forward. "Shut up!"

I chuckled at her reaction. "I'm serious. It happened in the elevator."

She covered her mouth with her hand, her eyes bugging out once more. "Oh my god, are you serious? What did you do?"

"What could I do?" I shrugged, still riding the high of the moment. "I enjoyed it."

"So, it's a good thing you texted him and not me then?"

"I don't know." I sank onto the couch beside her. "He told me to forget about the kiss."

"So he regrets it?"

"I don't know. Maybe. I think we're both trying to process what happened because it wasn't planned, you know?"

"Right."

We sat in silence for a moment until she asked, "Are you really going to forget about it?"

"Hell no. I literally can't stop thinking about it."

Sam grinned. "Well, whatever happens, just make sure it's worth it. You don't want to get fired over a kiss."

I rolled my eyes and swatted her playfully on the arm. "Thanks for the advice, Dr. Phil."

She laughed and nudged me with her elbow. "Hey, I'm just saying. You deserve to be happy, but not if it's going to cost you your job."

I smiled, grateful for her support. "I know, and I really appreciate it."

"Always."

Sam returned to her show, and I headed to my room for a quick shower. Except as I stood under the spray of the warm water, the thought of Sean's soft lips on mine was all I could think of as I soaped up my body.

Closing my eyes, I reached down and wrapped my hand around my hardening length. Images of him helping me stroke myself replaced memories of our kiss and caused me to moan as the water and the body wash helped my hand glide up and down my shaft.

Each stroke sent waves of pleasure coursing through me, and I pictured him before me on his knees. His eyes were dark with desire as his lips parted, waiting to take me into his warm mouth. My hips thrust as though I was fucking his gorgeous face.

Fucking my boss's gorgeous face.

"Yeah, Sean, you like that?" I breathed as I worked my cock. "You want this dick?" I jerked myself harder. "Yeah, you do. Take it into your mouth and suck."

My legs started to tremble, and I braced myself on the wall as I continued to work myself.

"Yeah, that's it."

With a ragged gasp, I let go, my cum coating the wall of the shower and leaving me spent.

I'd never spoken aloud while masturbating, never kissed an older man before, and never kissed my boss either, but damn, I was enjoying it all.

14

Sean

The following morning, I sat at my desk doing everything I could to delay joining Declan and Camille, who were already in the conference room working on the Whitman case.

How could I face the man I had not only kissed but had also pictured while I jerked off the night before? It was uncharted territory for me, and I didn't know how to handle working with someone I couldn't stop thinking about. When I couldn't put it off any longer, I grabbed my laptop and made my way down the hall.

"Good morning," I greeted as I entered the conference room.

Camille looked up from the stack of papers she was reviewing. "Good morning, Sean."

"Morning," Declan replied.

He wore a casual expression on his face, as if nothing had happened between us the night before. I wasn't sure if I was pleased or disappointed by his nonchalant attitude.

"How is the motion to suppress coming along? I have an appointment with my real estate agent this afternoon, so I'll be out of the office for a little while, and I'd like to get it filed with the court before I leave."

Camille passed a stack of papers over to me. "It's ready for your review. Once you give your approval, we'll be able to e-file it."

The three of us spent the next couple of hours discussing the upcoming trial, and I found myself stealing glances at Declan. His forehead wrinkled in concentration as he reviewed the documents in front of him. When my mind became fixated on the dark brown stubble that highlighted his kissable mouth, I could no longer deny that I was attracted to the man across from me. Despite what I'd said in the parking garage, I couldn't forget about our kiss.

At one o'clock, the alarm went off on my phone, reminding me I needed to leave to meet with my agent. "I'm going to head out, but I should be back in the next hour or so. You can call me if you need anything."

Declan gave me a head nod. "Got it, Bossman."

"See you soon," Camille added.

I double-checked the address for the condo and started walking in that direction. I'd already decided I wanted a place where I wouldn't have to drive to work every day, and this one would be a good test to see if that was feasible.

As I walked into the lobby of the condo building, my eyes scanned the sleek marble floors, the massive chandelier hanging from the ceiling, and the contemporary art adorning the walls. The place exuded luxury, but as I looked around, I didn't feel as though it really suited me.

Rita, my real estate agent, greeted me with a kind smile as she approached. "Sean, I'm glad you could escape the office for a little bit. I'm excited to show you this property," she said as she led me toward the elevator.

"Great. Let's take a look."

She rattled off the details while we rode up to the floor where the condo was located. "It has five bedrooms, seven baths, and spectacular views."

When we entered the condo, my jaw dropped at the sheer size of the place. While my house in Weston was much larger, I wasn't sure I needed so much space.

I followed Rita as she walked us through the open-concept living area and the kitchen I knew Jasper would love with the top-of-the-line appliances and a huge island. She continued on to the other rooms, pointing out all the features.

When we finished the tour, Rita asked, "So, what do you think?"

"Honestly, I don't believe this is the one. I think it's a little bigger than I'm looking for."

She nodded. "Okay. If you want less square footage, I have another place nearby that I can show you. It's still occupied, so I need to call the residents to schedule a time to show it. Would you be able to come see it this evening once you're done at the office if it works for them?"

"That should work fine. I'll see if one of my kids can come with me. I feel like I'm going to need a second opinion."

We walked into the hallway, and she locked up behind us. "Sounds good. I'll text you the address once I hear back from the owners."

"Thanks."

Once we exited the building, Rita headed toward her car, and I began walking back to my building. While waiting to cross the busy street, I pulled out my phone and sent Morgan a text.

> Are you available to maybe look at a condo with me tonight?

> Sorry. I can't. Going to a party

> On a Tuesday?

> Yes. Parties don't just happen on the weekends

Her message included a laughing emoji and an eye-rolling one.

> Okay. Have fun and be safe

I continued down the street and texted Ryan next.

> Do you have plans tonight? I might be looking at a condo and would like a second opinion

> Sorry Dad. I've got a work dinner to attend

Guess I was going to be on my own again.

> No problem. I'll let you know how it goes

When I arrived back at the office, I went straight to the conference room and found Declan working alone. "Hey, where's Camille?"

His head snapped up. "Oh, hey. She left to take a call."

I dropped into my chair and opened my laptop. "Anything important come up while I was gone?"

He shook his head. "Nope. I've just been reviewing some of the documents the prosecutor's office sent over recently. How was the condo?"

"Not great. It definitely wasn't the one for me. The problem is I'm not sure what exactly I'm looking for. I might look at another place this evening, so I asked my kids to go with me, but both are busy, so I might cancel."

"Don't do that. What if that place is your dream home?"

I shrugged. "It's just a little overwhelming. I've lived in the same house for twenty years, and this is a big change."

"What if I went with you?"

My eyes widened. "You want to go look at a condo with me?"

"Why not? I've got nothing else to do, and I've never been condo hunting before."

Spending time with Declan outside of the office was probably a bad idea, but that didn't stop me from agreeing. "Okay. I'll let you know what time as soon as I hear from my agent."

At six o'clock, Declan and I walked a few blocks to meet Rita. As we approached the building she'd sent me the information for, she was already waiting for us outside.

"Hello again, Sean. This must be your son."

Declan and I both laughed awkwardly at her assumption.

"Actually, my kids were both busy tonight. This is my coworker, Declan. Declan, this is Rita."

"Nice to meet you." Declan offered her his hand.

"Likewise." She shook his hand. "Now, let's head inside."

We entered the lobby, and Rita spoke to the man sitting at the concierge desk. "Peter, we're going to head up now."

He nodded as we passed him on our way to the elevator. When we stepped inside, she pressed the button for the twenty-fourth floor.

"Okay, you said you wanted something smaller than the last condo I showed you."

"Yeah, I definitely want to downsize."

"Well, this one has three bedrooms and two baths."

The elevator doors slid open, and we followed her down the hallway to the unit we were viewing. Once we stepped inside, I immediately noticed the difference between this place and the one I'd viewed earlier. It felt like an actual home, as opposed to a museum. But it still had all the modern amenities I could want.

"You need to check out this view," Declan announced as he looked out the floor-to-ceiling windows.

I stood beside him and could see both the downtown skyline and Boston Harbor. "Wow. This is amazing."

We continued to look around and eventually reached the primary bedroom. It was spacious, yet felt intimate at the same time. Or maybe it was because the man I'd fantasized about the night before was standing next to me.

The primary bedroom had access to a balcony that overlooked the city, and I could picture myself sitting on it with a glass of whisky to unwind after a long day.

We moved to the en suite, and someone clearly designed it with relaxation in mind. The marble countertops, the sleek glass shower, and the deep soaking tub were all white, while there were small teal details throughout the space.

Declan stepped into the walk-in shower and flashed a grin over his shoulder at me. "This thing could easily fit two people."

I felt a flush creep up my neck at his suggestive comment, and immediately, I remembered how his lips felt on mine. For a moment, I imagined what he would look like with hot water cascading over his naked body. I shook my head to rid it of the images I had no business imagining.

Rita walked in and asked, "So, what do you think? Was this closer to what you were looking for?"

"Yes, I think so."

"That's great. Just so you know, I don't expect this place to stay on the market much longer. If you're interested, you might not want to wait too long to put in an offer."

"Can I let you know in the morning?"

She smiled. "Absolutely."

We said our goodbyes, and then Declan and I began walking back to the office.

"Let me buy you dinner as a thank you for coming with me," I offered.

"I'm not going to say no to that."

"You want to grab a burger at The Backyard?" I asked, knowing the bar and grill was close by. Out of the handful of restaurants in the area, I thought it was best if we went somewhere casual.

"Burgers sound good to me."

We walked inside the establishment, and the host greeted us immediately. "Welcome. Table for two?"

"Yes," I answered.

"Do you want to sit at the bar, or would you like a table?"

I glanced at Declan and lifted an eyebrow. "Where do you want to sit?"

"Let's have a table."

"Okay, follow me." The host grabbed a couple of menus and led us through a maze of tables before seating us at one in the corner. "Your server will be with you shortly."

Declan and I sat across from each other and began looking over the menus before both of us decided on a barbecue bacon cheeseburger and fries.

After placing our order, Declan asked me, "So, what are you thinking about the condo?"

"I know I told Rita I need some time to think about it, but I really like it."

He leaned forward and placed his clasped hands on the table. "It has great views, and it's super close to work. Are you thinking about putting in an offer?"

I nodded and couldn't stop the smile that spread across my face. "I think so. I could definitely see myself living there."

"And that shower." He smirked.

I chuckled. "Yeah, that shower."

"I'm glad you found something."

"Thanks to you."

"Really?"

"Yeah. If you hadn't offered to go with me, I would have canceled my appointment and missed out on that place." I reached out and squeezed his hand.

The second we touched, the chemistry I had felt between us returned. I looked down and immediately pulled my hand back, not wanting to make things awkward between us. But when I looked up again, Declan's wide eyes told me he'd felt it too.

15

DECLAN

"Thank you again for dinner," I said as we walked toward the office.

"Thank you again for coming with me."

"I really enjoyed it. I probably will never be able to afford anything like that place, so it was fun."

"Why do you think that?" Sean asked as we stopped at an intersection.

I lifted a shoulder. "I don't know. I guess I'm just a long way from it."

He chuckled softly. "I didn't come from money either. I worked my tail off to build my reputation and build a profitable client list. It's allowed me to live my dreams and provide for my family and I know you can do it too."

"I totally get that, but it's just hard to imagine since I'm just starting out and all."

"I believe in you, Declan, and I can already tell you have what it takes to be just as successful as me, if not more."

His words made my heart smile. "Thanks. I needed to hear that."

As we reached the parking garage of our office building, we stopped next to his Porsche and faced each other.

There was a brief moment when I thought about leaning in for another kiss, but Sean spoke before I could act on it.

"Have a good night, Declan."

"You too, Sean."

He slid into his car, and I walked to Betsy a few rows over. The engine clicked as I turned the key but failed to start.

"Come on," I muttered, trying again with no success.

Just when I was about to give up hope, Betsy gave a sudden roar as she finally came to life. Relief flooded through me and I blew out a breath, but I had a feeling old Betsy was about to keel over.

With the engine rumbling, I backed out of the parking space and headed home. As I pulled into the parking lot of my apartment building, my phone buzzed in my pocket. I glanced at the screen to see my mom's name.

"Hey, Mom," I answered as I stepped out of the car.

"Declan, sweetheart, how was your day?"

"It was good," I replied, walking toward the building. "Went to dinner with my boss."

"Just the two of you?"

"Yeah." I rubbed the back of my neck. "He needed help with something and then wanted to say thank you with dinner."

"That's wonderful," she replied, sounding genuinely pleased. "Are you still having to work late hours?"

"Sometimes."

"Just make sure you're not letting work consume all your time, Declan. It's important to maintain a healthy work-life balance."

"I know, Mom," I reassured her as I slid my key into the lock. She had worked three jobs when I was a kid and I knew she felt as though she missed out on so much when it came to me. I supposed she didn't want the same for me, but I wasn't going to argue with her. "But if I want him to promote me once I pass the bar, I need to do whatever he asks."

"I just worry about you."

"And I worry about you." I walked into the quiet, empty apartment.

"Me?"

I nodded and closed the door behind me. "You're on your feet all day at the diner. You need to relax too."

"I've been working there for over twenty years. My body is used to it."

"Well, once I make associate money, I want to get you a nicer place to live."

"A nicer place?"

"Yeah, like an apartment or something."

"Oh, sweetheart. You know I don't mind living in a trailer. Have for my entire life."

I sat on the couch and rested my head against the back. "Still. When I can afford it, I'm going to get you a place with a pool or something."

She chuckled softly. "A pool?"

"Yeah. Apartments have pools."

"I know, but what's special about a pool?"

"I don't know, but wouldn't it be nice to lie by one and enjoy the sun?"

"Absolutely."

"See? That's what I want for you."

"Sweetheart, it's not your job to provide for me."

"I know that, but I want to." I sighed.

"We'll see. You still have bills of your own. Plus, you can't live with Sam forever."

"I won't be. I went with my boss to look at a condo he's thinking about buying and seeing what he could afford sparked something in me. One day, we're going to live in a place looking over the river."

"We're? You mean me and you?"

"Yeah."

"Declan, sweetheart—"

"Just let me do this for you."

"We'll see."

"Fine." I rolled my eyes.

"All right. I won't keep you any longer. I just wanted to check in."

"I appreciate it, Mom. I'll talk to you soon, okay?"

"Okay, sweetheart. Love you."

"Love you too."

I hung up and walked toward where Sam and I kept our alcohol. Not that the conversation with my mom was bad, but I really wanted to drink. Except as I reached for the Tito's, I realized I didn't want to drink alone. I sent Fallon a text.

> Want to grab a drink?

I went to my room to change out of my button-up and slacks. Fallon responded, as I slipped on a pair of jeans.

> Yeah, got the approval. Where?

> IDK. Either Chrome or Flanagan's I guess

> Is Sam working?

> Yeah

> Then let's do Flanagan's unless you're looking to hook up tonight

> Flanagan's is fine

> Ok. We'll pick you up in 30

After I got ready, I waited another five minutes and Fallon texted he was downstairs. Grabbing my keys, wallet, and phone, I headed out to meet him. Rhett stood by the open back door of the black SUV, dressed in his Secret Service suit.

"How's it going?" I asked him.

"Good, Dec. You?"

"No complaints. Thanks for letting your husband come out last minute."

"Do you really think I could stop him?"

I snorted a laugh and slid in next to Fallon in the back seat. "No, but I'd bet you two would have fun if you tried."

"Stop flirting with my husband," Fallon teased playfully.

"Aw come on. You know he only has eyes for you."

"I do know that." Fallon smirked.

Fallon talked about a few cases he was working on before the SUV pulled up outside Flanagan's. After Rhett and his guys did their sweep of the bar, Rhett opened the door, and Fallon and I slid out of the vehicle. We made our way inside, where Sam was busy mixing drinks and serving customers. She looked up as we approached, a welcoming smile lighting up her face.

"Hey, boys." She wiped her hands on a towel. "What can I get you?"

Fallon ordered a beer, and I hesitated for a moment before replying, "A vodka soda for me, thanks."

Once she handed them over, Fallon and I went to the table Rhett had snagged for us and we settled in.

"So, how's Ashford, Nolan & Torrance?" Fallon asked, taking a sip of his beer.

I took a gulp of my drink. I had been hoping we would avoid details about my office life. "It's good."

Fallon arched a brow. "Good? That's all you've got?"

I hesitated, unsure of how much to reveal. But then, I figured what the hell, Fallon was one of my closest friends.

"It's Sean," I confessed quietly. "Things between us have become ... complicated."

Fallon's eyebrows shot up in surprise. "Complicated how?"

I took a deep breath, trying to gather my thoughts. "Well, for starters, we kissed."

Fallon's eyes widened in shock. "You kissed my uncle?"

I nodded, feeling a knot forming in my stomach. "I thought things between us would be weird, but they aren't. I went condo hunting with him today and—"

"Wait. You two went condo hunting?"

"Yeah. His kids couldn't make it and he wanted someone else's opinion because he wants to sell his house and move closer to the office."

"Wow. I had no idea."

"And—"

"But hold up. You kissed?"

I grimaced slightly and looked off to the side. "Maybe?"

"How the hell did that happen? He's straight."

"You keep telling me that, but I'm not so sure."

"He was married and has kids," Fallon stated, as though I didn't know.

"Come on, baby boy. You know how I have Poppy," Rhett chimed in from where he stood behind Fallon.

"I have never known him to be into guys," Fallon clarified.

"Maybe it's just me." I smirked, liking that idea.

"Okay, but he is also your boss."

"I know." I sighed. "That's why it's complicated. He put the brakes on, and I totally get it."

"It's probably for the best."

Maybe Fallon was right, but I liked the time I was spending with Sean when it was just the two of us. "Maybe, but don't say anything, okay?"

"Of course not. That's his business, not mine."

"Thanks."

After a few drinks, Fallon and I called it a night. Rhett and his guys drove us back to my apartment building, then dropped me off with a quick wave.

Alone once again, I let out a tired sigh and trudged up the stairs to my apartment. As I stepped inside and closed the door behind me, my mind was once again fixed on Sean. No man had ever consumed my thoughts the way he was, and it sucked because we couldn't be more. Or at least, he said we couldn't be more. He was the one who had said we needed to forget the kiss, and as far as he knew, I had.

But, of course, I hadn't.

I kicked off my shoes and made my way to the kitchen to grab a bottle of water. My phone vibrated in my pocket, and I thought I would see a text from Fallon, but it was from Sean. My eyes widened as I read the message.

> I know it's late, but I just wanted to say thanks again for this afternoon. I couldn't wait and submitted an offer. I truly appreciated your help today. Have a great night. See you tomorrow

I felt no hesitation as I sent back:

> Anytime. Hope you get the place and have a good night too. See you in the morning

Two Months Later

Late in the afternoon, I sat at my desk, engrossed in writing a brief when my email chimed. I had been trying to forget that it was the day Fallon and I would learn if we'd passed the bar, but I had failed completely and could think of nothing else most of the day. Since nine a.m., I had refreshed my email over and over as if that would make the results come faster.

With my heart pounding, I clicked on the email tab on the browser and my gaze went straight to the new email that had come in. The subject line read: "Official Results, Massachusetts July Bar Exam"

"Oh, fuck," I murmured.

With a shaky hand, I opened the email. My eyes scanned the text, searching for the words that would determine my future.

Dear Applicant for Admission to the Bar in Massachusetts,
 Congratulations! The Board of Bar Examiners is pleased to inform you that you obtained a passing total scaled score ...

"I did it! I passed the bar exam!" I exclaimed, jumping out of my chair and throwing my arms into the air.

Cheers erupted as my coworkers gathered around me, offering their congratulations and slapping me on the back. But one person stood out as he waited his turn. Without a word, Sean pulled me into a tight embrace.

"Congratulations, Declan," he murmured against my ear, and a shiver ran down my spine.

"Thank you."

We pulled apart.

"When you get the notice from the court for the date and time of your formal admission ceremony, let me know. I want to be there."

"Absolutely."

"Do you know if Fallon passed?" he asked.

I shook my head, but turned back to my desk and sat. "No, but I might be able to look it up."

I went to the website for the Commonwealth of Massachusetts and pulled up the pass list for the bar exam. Clicking on the last names that started with C-D, I scrolled to Donnelley and there he was: Donnelley, Fallon James – Boston MA.

Spinning around, I said to Sean, "He passed too."

"Excellent news. You two are going to make exceptional attorneys."

"Thank you."

Sean turned and left. I grabbed my phone and shot a text to Fallon:

> Well?

I didn't want to spoil it for him if he hadn't checked his email yet. A few seconds later he responded:

> I passed. You?

> I passed too!

> Drinks tonight?

Fuck yeah!

16

Sean

Finishing up my work for the week, I debated whether I should join the rest of the office who had left thirty minutes ago to celebrate Declan's admission to the bar. I had attended the ceremony, but then returned to the office to get some work done. I rarely went out with my employees for happy hour because I believed they deserved to relax and chat openly without worrying about their boss hearing everything they said. But this was a special night for Declan, and everyone had been invited.

It had been a few months since we had kissed in the elevator and looked at the condo together, and our relationship had moved back into a strictly professional one. I didn't know if that was because I'd told him we had to pretend as though nothing happened between us or because we were buried under a mountain of work.

Whatever the reason, I missed our non-work-related conversations like the ones we had shared around the fire in Cape Cod or when we'd gone to dinner. And I didn't know what that meant for me.

Did I see Declan as a friend and someone I wanted to hang out with? Or was there more? I was pretty certain it was the latter, but I still had difficulty wrapping my head around the fact that the first person I felt I might be interested in since my wife died was a man. However, I couldn't deny I was drawn to him in a way I hadn't been to another person since Melinda.

After a few more minutes of considering what I should do, I decided to go celebrate with everyone because I wanted Declan to know I was happy about his recent accomplishment. Just like I had told him on the day we'd gone to look at the condo—which I was closing on next week—I believed in him. His work ethic and drive were impeccable, and I had no doubt he was going to be a very prominent attorney one day.

Leaving my stuff in my office to get later, I locked up and made my way to the restaurant down the street. As I walked into The Backyard, I quickly spotted the group from Ashford, Nolan & Torrance taking up a large portion of the bar area.

"Hey, Sean." Camille waved me over even though I was already walking in her direction.

Declan's head whipped up, and a smile spread across his face when he saw me. "Bossman, I didn't know you were coming tonight."

I clapped him on the shoulder as I stepped up beside him. "I wasn't going to miss celebrating you passing the bar." Noticing he didn't have a drink in front of him, I announced to the group, "Next round is on me."

The other employees cheered, and I handed the bartender my credit card, ordering two bottles of Stella Artois at the same time. I gave one of the beers to Declan and said, "Congratulations. There was never a doubt in my mind you'd pass."

"Thanks, Sean." He took the bottle from me, and we moved over to a high-top table to make room for the others to place their orders. "I'm glad you were confident I'd pass. When I left the exam, I wasn't so sure." He took a sip of his beer. "How'd you know what kind of beer I liked?"

Telling him I remembered what he'd ordered at Fallon's wedding seemed not only weird but like I was admitting something I wasn't ready to put words to. Instead, I shrugged. "Lucky guess."

"Thanks for the drink, Sean," Clark, a junior associate, called out, and I raised my bottle in acknowledgment.

I shifted my focus back to Declan. "Now that you're an official lawyer, I need to have a chat about your job with the other partners."

He smiled. "I hope it will be a good chat."

I gave him a matching grin. "I'm sure it will be."

Camille joined us with a bright green drink in her hand, and several others soon followed her. The conversation quickly switched to everyone's plans for the upcoming weekend.

"What about you, Sean?" Declan asked. "Got any exciting plans?"

"Not really. Probably just packing. I'm supposed to move into my new place next weekend."

Camille gave me a questioning look. "You're not hiring movers?"

"I am, but I'm also downsizing, so I need to finish going through stuff and decide what I'm keeping and what I can get rid of."

"Moving is the worst," Clark interjected.

"Yeah, it's been a lot of work so far. But I am looking forward to having practically zero commute."

"Plus, that shower's totally worth it," Declan muttered under his breath, so only I could hear him.

Once again, I found myself thinking about him standing naked under the water. I needed to get a grip and stop indulging in inappropriate thoughts about my employee.

A couple of hours later, everyone except Declan, Camille, and me had left.

"Well, guys. I need to call it a night. The kids get up early, even on the weekends," Camille stated.

"See you Monday," I said as she stood.

"Thanks for getting everyone to come out tonight." Declan hugged her.

"Congratulations again," she said, and then she left.

Declan turned to me. "I'm going to close my tab and head out too."

A slight pang of disappointment hit me, knowing the night was ending. "Yeah, I should do the same."

We stepped up to the bar, and the bartender came over, flashing a smile at Declan. "You want another drink, handsome?" she asked.

He shook his head. "Nah, we're both heading out."

The bartender gave me a quick glance and then turned her attention back to Declan. "Are you calling it a night or going somewhere else?"

"Just going home."

She settled our tabs and handed us our receipts to sign. "I get off in an hour if you're not ready to call it a night."

Declan smiled. "Ah, thanks. But I think I'm going to pass. It's been a long week."

She wrote something down on his receipt and slid it to Declan. "There's my number if you change your mind."

"Here you go." I pushed the restaurant copy of my receipt across the bar with a little more force than necessary and then turned to Declan. "Ready?"

"Uh ... sure."

I spun on my heel and weaved through the tables and out the door.

"What was that all about?" Declan asked once we were outside.

I couldn't believe I let my jealousy show. Especially when I knew he wasn't interested in her. But even if it had been a guy who'd caught Declan's eye, he could do whatever he wanted. It wasn't as though anything was going on between us that would or should stop him.

I couldn't admit to him I'd been jealous, so I said, "Just didn't want her to feel bad when you turned down her offer again."

He chuckled. "I'm sure she would have been okay."

"Probably." I shrugged. "And I shouldn't have stepped in."

"No worries. It was a little awkward having her hit on me in front of you."

I didn't know how to respond, but we were already back at our building. I was about to tell him to have a good weekend when he followed me to the elevator. "Are you going up to the office?"

"Yeah. I need to grab my things."

"Okay. I left my stuff there too."

As soon as the elevator doors closed behind us, I couldn't stop thinking about the kiss we'd shared inside the confined space. I glanced at Declan from the corner of my eye, wondering if he was also remembering the moment.

Fortunately—or maybe it was unfortunate—the elevator didn't have any problems, and once on our floor, we headed toward Declan's desk.

"I'm going to grab my stuff, and then I'll walk out with you," I said and hurried to my office, not waiting for his response. Not bothering to turn on my lights, I grabbed my briefcase and spun around to leave, only to find Declan leaning in the doorway. "You ready to go?" I asked.

He pushed off the doorframe and closed the door behind him. "In a minute. But first, I need to ask you a question."

"Okay?"

He moved toward me. "Were you really trying to protect the bartender's feelings back there, or were you jealous?"

My pulse raced as I thought about my answer. "I don't know what you're talking about."

"Are you sure?" He smirked. "Because I didn't miss the look you threw my way in the elevator. And if I had to guess, you were thinking about our kiss."

I swallowed. "I may have been thinking about it."

"Were you thinking about doing it again?"

There was no point in lying. "Yes."

He stepped closer until our shoes were touching. The way his breath felt on my lips made me want to kiss him again as we had weeks ago. But I didn't. I waited for him to make the first move. Maybe it was because I was his boss, and I wanted to give him a chance to stop whatever we were doing, or perhaps I was just too chicken to take what I wanted.

Thankfully, I didn't have to wait long for him to capture my lips with his. A second later, he ran his tongue over the seam of my mouth, and I opened for him so he could deepen the kiss. As our tongues continued dancing together, he trailed his hand down my arm and across my abs before cupping the quickly growing bulge behind my pants.

I remembered picturing the exact situation when I first jerked off while thinking about our elevator encounter, but the reality was a hundred times better than the fantasy.

Moaning into his mouth, I placed my hand over his, urging him to grip me harder.

He pulled away, and his eyes sparkled in the dim light from outside. "Do you want me to keep going?"

It surprised me he took the time to ask, but I nodded. "I do."

"Good, because there's something I've been wanting to do for a while."

My pulse spiked as I watched him drop to his knees and begin unbuckling my belt. His moves were slow and deliberate, making my anticipation almost too much to bear. Once my belt was out of the way, he undid the button and lowered the zipper of my slacks before pushing them and my underwear down to my knees.

There I stood in the middle of my office with my dick standing at attention, waiting for my employee to blow me. It wasn't too late for me to put a stop to things. I probably needed to. Maybe even should have. Yet, I couldn't seem to speak those words. All I could think about was how good it would feel when he finally wrapped his lips around me.

"Fuck, you have a perfect dick," Declan praised as he stroked me a few times.

Groaning, I braced myself on the desk behind me and closed my eyes. A second later, I felt his tongue lick a path up the underside of my shaft from balls to tip. I tightened my grip on the edge of my desk, savoring the sensation. He swirled his tongue around my crown a few times and then took my entire length into his mouth.

My eyes flew open, and I let out a long moan. "My god, your mouth feels amazing."

He waggled his eyebrows in response but didn't pull off my cock to reply. Instead, he began bobbing his head as his mouth and hand worked in tandem to bring me pleasure.

Everything about it felt forbidden. Maybe that was why it didn't take me long to utter the words, "I'm going to come."

Instead of pulling away after my warning like I'd thought he might, he took me deeper, and a second later, I was shooting my cum down his throat. When nothing remained for him to swallow, he sat back and beamed at me.

Needing to touch him, I ran my thumb over his bottom lip. "What are you doing to me?"

17

DECLAN

I looked up at Sean and licked my lips. "What am I doing to you? I can ask the same about you."

"You have to know I don't normally do this."

I stood while he tucked himself back into his pants. "Do you mean with men, your employees, someone younger, or what?"

"All the above."

"Did you enjoy it, though?"

He turned away as if he were embarrassed. "I did, but—"

I reached out and grabbed his arm to stop him from walking away. "No, buts, Sean. We're adults."

"But you're my employee."

I let go of his arm and took a step closer to him. "Okay, but I haven't read anywhere that it's against company policy to date within the office, so is it because I'm a guy?"

He glanced at my lips and then back up to my eyes. I wanted to grab his hand, but I thought better of it.

"Like I said, it's everything. All of this is new to me." He took a step back and looked out at the twinkling city lights.

I moved behind him and rested my chin on his shoulder. "We can take things slow. No one needs to know but us."

He turned, and we looked into each other's eyes, neither one of us turning away. "And what if someone finds out?"

"If you don't have an issue with it, then we can deal with it if that happens, but I really see no problem because we're both consenting adults."

"You make it sound so simple," he whispered.

I tilted my head, our lips mere inches apart. "Maybe it can be."

Without hesitation, I closed the gap between us, pressing my lips to his. It felt like everything fell into place at that moment, like we'd sealed our relationship with a kiss.

When we pulled apart, Sean said, "We should head out before the cleaning crew gets here."

I nodded, reluctantly stepping back. "Yeah, I'm supposed to meet Fallon."

Sean grabbed his briefcase. "Tell him congrats for me again."

"You know, you could come." I smirked.

"Come where?"

In my mouth again. "I'm meeting him at Chrome."

"What is Chrome?"

"A gay nightclub."

Sean shook his head slowly. "I don't know."

"All right. If you change your mind, you know where I'll be."

Except he didn't change his mind and instead, I partied the night away with Fallon and some more friends to celebrate that he and I were finally attorneys at law.

MONDAY MORNING, I HAD THE USUAL PEP IN MY STEP AS I STEPPED OUT of the elevator and into the office. I set my stuff down on my desk and peeked over my shoulder to see Sean's office door was closed. The light was on, so I knew he was inside.

Despite agreeing to see where things went between us, we hadn't spoken since Friday night. I'd wanted to reach out and text him, but I didn't because I knew he was still on the fence about everything. He needed to be the one to make the next move.

"Good morning, Camille. How was your weekend?" I asked as I looked over at her cubicle.

"It was good, but busy. Went to my son's football game, did some laundry, and cleaned the apartment. You know how it goes. How was your weekend?"

"Did those same things minus football."

"You didn't even watch the New England game last night?"

I shook my head. "Watching sports on TV isn't really my thing."

"That's a shame. I thought you'd be into the tight pants."

"Tight pants, you say?" I chuckled.

Camille laughed. "See? You're missing out."

"Well, maybe I'll check out these tight pants."

"Just wait for baseball season. They're even better without all the pads blocking their muscles."

Before I could respond, Sean's door opened, and he called out, "Declan. My office."

Camille and I shared a look and then I hurried to his office. He wasn't alone.

"Yes, sir?"

Sean's gaze heated at my words, but he quickly recovered and gestured to the open chair between Luke Nolan and Eli Torrance. "Have a seat."

I took the seat Sean indicated. Luke and Eli were both partners of the firm and seeing them in Sean's office alongside him meant it wasn't going to be an ordinary morning meeting. Had he told them we fooled around, and he wanted not to keep the secret from the firm? It wasn't as though Luke's affair was public knowledge. Though I was certain everyone in the office knew, people kept it hush-hush because Luke was married.

"Declan," Sean began as he took his seat on the other side of the desk. "I hope you had a good weekend."

"It was all right," I replied, trying to keep my tone steady despite the butterflies swirling in my stomach.

"You weren't drunk the entire time while celebrating?" Luke asked.

"Only Friday night." I looked across at Sean. "Don't remember getting back to my place, to be honest."

Sean cleared his throat. "Well, we're glad you're safe and at work today."

"Thanks." I smiled a small smile.

Sean continued. "We've called you in here because, as you know, I've been observing your work closely over the past few months, and I'm impressed with your dedication and diligence. Your commitment to the cases you've worked on hasn't gone unnoticed."

I felt a surge of pride wash over me at his words, but I kept my expression neutral, not wanting to show too much emotion just yet. "Thank you."

"And," Sean went on, "as we've discussed previously, we're pleased officially to promote you to junior associate, effective immediately."

A rush of excitement coursed through me, threatening to break through the calm facade I'd been trying to maintain. This was the moment I'd been eagerly awaiting since starting law school.

"Thank you all." I beamed. "Happy to be an attorney officially for Ashford, Nolan & Torrance."

We all stood, and the three men shook my hand. Luke and Eli went for the door, and I followed behind them until Sean said, "Declan. Have a minute to discuss the Barker case?"

"Of course." I turned back around.

Once the other partners were gone, Sean closed his door. We stood facing each other, and I was seconds from kissing him, but I had to wait for his move.

"You had a good weekend?" he asked me again.

"It would have been better if I'd seen you."

"Sorry." He cupped my face with one hand and brushed my cheek with his thumb before pulling away. "I was busy packing. Still not done, and I'm moving this weekend."

"You know, I'm a really good packer."

"Oh, yeah?" He chuckled.

I nodded with a grin.

"Well, in that case," Sean said, closing the distance between us even more, "how about you come over to my place after work today? I could definitely use some help, and it would give us a chance to ... catch up about your weekend."

I couldn't help but smile at his suggestion. "I'd love to. Consider me your packing assistant for the evening."

"Great." There was a hint of excitement in his eyes. "It's a date then."

Warmth raced through me at the word 'date', and before I could think twice, I leaned in and pressed my lips against his. There was only a brief slip of his tongue before he pulled away, but instead of being the we-can't-do-this Sean, he was smiling from ear to ear.

"I'll see you after work at my house." His voice was low and husky.

"I'll be counting down the minutes."

With one last glance and a shared smile, I turned and headed back to my desk, unable to wipe the grin off my face. It was definitely shaping up to be a good day.

SEAN LEFT THE OFFICE BEFORE I DID BUT HAD TEXTED ME HIS address. He was stopping to grab pizza and beer before I was to meet him. I let a good fifteen minutes pass before I stood and grabbed my things.

"Leaving already?" Camille asked as she glanced at her watch. "First day as an official attorney and you're hightailing it out of here before six."

"Have a date." I beamed, telling her the truth.

Her eyes widened. "Oh, really? On a Monday?"

"Beggars can't be choosers." I winked and started for the elevators. "See ya tomorrow."

"Good luck!"

Once I was in the parking garage, I hurried toward Betsy, threw my bag onto the passenger seat, and slid inside. After buckling my seatbelt, I cranked the engine.

Nothing happened.

"Oh, you've got to be kidding me today, girl. Don't do this to your boy." I tried again, but all it did was click. I rubbed the dashboard. "If you just get me to Sean's house, I'll give you premium gas the next time I fill you up." I gave her a little pat and turned the key again. She sputtered to life, and I sighed. "Thank you. Premium gas is in your future."

I backed out of the space and headed to the address Sean had texted me. Forty minutes and several spots of heavy traffic later, I pulled into the driveway and parked in front of the three-car garage.

His house was huge. Even though I knew he was rich, it still surprised me as I walked up to the front of the three-story home.

The thought of spending the evening with Sean, helping him pack for his move while enjoying pizza and beer, was enough to make any Monday feel like a Friday.

I knocked on the door, and it swung open. Sean stood in the entry with a warm smile on his face. "Hey there," he greeted, stepping aside to let me in. "Long time no see."

"Yeah." I chuckled, moving inside and taking in the grand foyer packed with moving boxes. "I actually almost had to cancel."

"Why?"

"Betsy didn't start the first few times I tried."

"Have you had a mechanic look at her?"

"She needs a new engine, and I might as well get a new car."

Sean led me to the living room, where a large pizza box sat on the coffee table alongside a couple of bottles of Stella.

"Now that you're getting a raise, maybe you can."

"I'm not sure. I want to move my mom into a better place before I get a new car."

He gestured to the pizza. "Help yourself. I hope you like pepperoni."

"Love it," I replied, grabbing a slice and a bottle of beer.

He opened the cap for me and handed the bottle back. "And thanks for helping me pack. I had no idea how much shit I had until I started going through everything. I've had to buy more boxes four different times."

"Of course. Is all of it going to fit into your new place?"

Sean shook his head while he grabbed a slice of pizza. "No. My son and daughter are taking some stuff. Other stuff I'm giving away."

"Will it be weird for you to live in a new place?"

He took a bite before responding. "I'm sure it will be, but it's time. We bought this house when our kids were still in elementary school and now that it's just me, I don't need all of this space."

I settled onto the plush couch. "Well, at least you won't have to worry about the upkeep of such a massive home all by yourself, right?"

"You've got a point there. It definitely keeps me busy, but I suppose it's a small price to pay for all this space."

"The joys of being a homeowner."

He took a sip of beer. "Speaking of homes, do you ever envision filling one with a family of your own someday?"

His question caught me off guard, but I rolled with it. "Hmm, sometimes I do. It's definitely something I've thought about, but it all depends on finding the right partner and being in the right place in life. Since I just became an attorney, I want to focus on my career for now."

Sean nodded. "Yeah, it's a big decision. When I got my first job, we already had Ryan, and Melinda was pregnant with Morgan. It was tough. Rough on her too, since she was home with them by herself while I worked a lot of late nights."

"You still work long hours though, so that doesn't change?"

"It all depends on your caseload."

"True." I bit into the greasy goodness. "I guess we'll see. If it works out, it works out."

The front door opened suddenly, and I heard a female's voice call out, "Dad?"

Sean's eyes widened as he looked over at me. "In the living room, honey."

Morgan rounded the corner and smiled. "I thought that was your beater out front, Declan. What are you doing here?"

"I … ah …" I couldn't find the words.

"He offered to help me pack, unlike you," Sean stated.

"I told you you should have hired someone to do that. Or did you hire Declan?"

"Like I said, he offered to help, but why are you here?" He stood and hugged her.

"I'm going to this Roaring 20s party on Saturday and came to get some of Mom's jewelry."

"You know she wanted you to have it all."

"I know." She shrugged slightly. "I'll be up in your room getting it."

"You're not going to stay and help us pack?" Sean asked. "Moving day is Saturday."

Morgan balked. "Help pack? Yeah, no. Have fun with that."

She turned and walked up the stairs, I asked Sean in a low voice, "Should I leave?"

"No, but maybe we should get to packing."

18

Sean

Morgan left not long after she stopped by, but Declan and I spent a couple hours packing up my home office. I didn't want the movers messing with my files and the other things I had in there. Besides, it would ensure everything stayed organized until I was able to set up my office in my new place.

"What's next?" Declan asked as he stacked the last box on top of the others near the door.

"I think I'm going to call it a night." I stretched my arms over my head, my sweater rising slightly to reveal part of my stomach. "This old man needs a break."

He let his gaze travel up and down my body. "You look like you're doing just fine."

Having a guy half my age compliment me was a boost to my ego, and I'd be lying if I said I didn't enjoy him checking me out. It gave me an idea.

"I think I'm going to relax in my hot tub for a bit. Do you want to join me?"

"You have a hot tub?"

I nodded. "Yeah. I think it might be what I'll miss most about this place."

"Well, I'd love to go out there, but I didn't bring anything to wear in a hot tub."

"Boxers work."

He grinned. "Then let's go."

I led him downstairs, and I heard him gasp when we entered my home gym.

"No wonder you look the way you do. You've got everything in here."

I glanced around the space, taking note of the various machines and free weights that I ended up selling with the place. "Thank goodness the new place has a gym. Gotta make sure I don't let myself go." I winked.

Declan bit his lip, and if he kept looking at me the way he was, we weren't going to make it out to the hot tub.

"C'mon, let's go outside." I walked into the mudroom and grabbed some towels from the cabinet. "We can leave our clothes in here."

"Are you going out in your underwear too?"

I shrugged. "Why not?"

"Okay."

I watched unabashedly while he stripped out of his clothes. While I appreciated what he looked like in a button-up shirt with the sleeves rolled up and his tailored dress pants, nothing compared to seeing him in just his navy blue boxers.

"Shouldn't you be getting undressed too? Or are you just going to stare at me all night?" He smirked.

"As tempting as that sounds, the hot water is calling my name."

I made quick work of my clothes, picked up the towels, and headed to the back yard. I placed the towels on one of the lounge chairs and then stepped into the steaming water. Slipping under the water until it went past my shoulders, I let out a long sigh.

"Feels that good?" Declan asked.

"Get in here and find out for yourself."

Instead of getting in across from where I was, he sat directly beside me. Once he was seated, I turned on the jets and sank even lower.

"This is amazing," he said, looking up at the bright stars above us.

"It is," I agreed.

We sat in silence for a little while, our eyes closed as we let the hot water relax our muscles.

Eventually, Declan said, "I now understand why you enjoy this so much. I'd give anything to have a hot tub at my apartment complex."

"It's a great stress release," I agreed.

"You know what else is good at relieving stress?"

Before I could respond, he leaned over and kissed me. Immediately, my tongue sought out his as I wrapped my arms around his neck and pulled him closer. He slipped his hand into my boxer briefs and rubbed my aching dick.

"I really want to suck you off again."

I groaned. "Fuck. I'd like that."

After the chat that followed the amazing blow job he gave me in my office, any confusion I had about my feelings toward Declan had disappeared. He was smart, ambitious, and sexy as hell. And I knew it would be stupid of me if I ignored my attraction to him simply because of his gender. Besides everyone had been telling me I needed to live my life, so that was what I was going to do.

"It's cold out here. Maybe we should go back inside," he suggested.

"Yeah." I nipped his chin and then moved back to his lips. Even though I hadn't gotten my fill of kissing him, I forced myself to pull away because I wanted to feel his mouth on me again more than anything. "Let's go."

We raced across the backyard, and as soon as the mudroom door closed behind us, Declan knelt in front of me and quickly pulled off my soaking-wet underwear. He grabbed my hips and engulfed my cock until I hit the back of his throat.

"Holy shit. Are you trying to kill me?" I bent forward and held onto his shoulders.

He pulled off of my shaft with an audible pop. "Nope. Just trying to make you come."

He went back to sucking me deep and then pushed on my ass, encouraging me to thrust into his mouth. I moved my hands from his shoulders to the back of his head and began moving. I watched him for any clue my movements were too much for him, but all he did was moan loudly around my cock.

I could feel myself getting close, but before I could say anything, he swallowed, and I felt his throat constrict around my tip. That was all it took for me to shout, "Fuck," as I came.

When my dick stopped pulsing, I pulled out of his mouth, and he licked his lips.

"That was so good," I breathed.

He smirked. "And you're still alive."

"That I am." I chuckled.

Once he was back on his feet, he pulled off his wet boxers, giving me a peek at what he was packing, and pulled on his pants. "I hate to blow and go, but it's getting late, so I should probably head out."

I choked on a laugh. "You're ridiculous."

He shrugged. "Yeah, but you like it."

He wasn't wrong. Being around him brought out the fun side of me that I'd kept tucked away for too long.

"I guess I do," I admitted as we both finished getting dressed.

He smiled, and I walked with him to my door.

"Thanks for coming over tonight," I said as we stepped outside. "I definitely needed your help."

"Anytime." He unlocked his car door and then looked up at me. "See you tomorrow."

Staring into his dark brown eyes, I leaned forward. It was the first time I had initiated a kiss between us, but I'd been wanting to do it. When our lips met, I traced the seam of his mouth with my tongue. Immediately, he opened to me, and I deepened the kiss. Cupping his face with my hands, I marveled at the feel of his short stubble against my palms. It was different from anything I'd felt before, but I liked it.

His lips were soft, yet his mouth held a hint of dominance, and I couldn't seem to get enough of him.

When we finally broke apart, I said, "Have a good night."

"You too." He climbed into the driver's seat, put the bag with his wet boxers in the passenger seat, and closed the door.

He tried to start his car, but the only sound it made was a clicking noise, and then nothing happened.

"Shit," he groaned, trying it again and getting the same result.

I opened the door and asked, "Is that the same thing it was doing when you left work?"

He nodded and tried one more time. "Yeah. Unfortunately, I don't think she's going to start this time." He got out of his car and slammed the door. "Guess I need to call a tow truck."

"Let's go back inside then."

He followed me into the house, and I offered him a bottle of water while he searched on his phone for a local towing company. It took him calling a few places before he finally found one that could have a truck help in less than an hour.

"Are you going to have them tow it to your place?" I asked after he hung up.

"No. There's a repair shop I've used a few times. I'll have the driver take it there."

"What are you going to do in the meantime?"

He shrugged. "I'll either take The T or use a rideshare."

An idea popped into my head. "I've got an SUV you can borrow until you get your car fixed."

"I can't use your car," he argued.

"Why not? It's just sitting in the garage."

"You have an extra vehicle you don't use?"

I didn't plan on mentioning the Cadillac Escalade had been Melinda's vehicle. It wasn't as though I was keeping it around because it held sentimental value. Rather, it was a great second car to have, especially when we headed to the mountains to go skiing. But since he asked, I felt as though I should give him an answer. "It was my wife's, and I don't use it often."

"Oh ... Are you sure you're okay with me borrowing it?"

"Absolutely. Let me go grab the key."

Once I pulled the spare key out of the drawer, I nodded my head toward the garage, and Declan followed me.

"That's quite a bit bigger than Betsy," he stated.

I looked over at the white SUV. "Is that okay?"

"Yeah, I can handle big equipment." He smirked.

"I'm sure you can." I laughed. "You want to check it out?"

He took the key from my outstretched hand and opened the door. "Seriously, this is really nice of you. I'm going to owe you big time."

"We can work something out later."

He grinned. "If you're asking for sexual favors because you're helping me—"

My eyes widened as I shook my head. "No. That's not what I'm saying."

He barked out a laugh. "I was going to say that sounded like a good deal to me."

"You're too much." I chuckled.

"You like it."

"I do," I admitted.

He slid into the driver's seat and pressed the button to start the engine. "It starts on the first try? That's going to take some getting used to."

"I think that's something you'll adjust to quickly," I teased.

"Probably." He looked at the time on the display. "I hope the tow truck gets here soon. I didn't mean to keep you up this late."

"I don't mind. If you want to take off, I can give the driver the address for the repair shop."

"You're okay with that?"

"I wouldn't have offered if I wasn't. That way, you can go home and get some sleep." By letting me deal with the tow truck, he'd get home about thirty minutes sooner than he would if he waited for it.

"Okay. Here's the key." He took the key to his car off his key ring and handed it over before leaning forward to press a soft kiss to my lips. "Thank you."

"You're welcome." I took a step back so he could close the door.

I watched as he reversed out of the garage and saw him give me a small wave as he drove off.

THE WEEK PASSED BY IN A BLUR AS I SPENT MORE TIME IN COURT THAN I did in the office. That meant Declan and I only saw each other in passing over the past five days.

When I finally returned to the office Friday evening, he was gone, along with everyone else. Knowing I couldn't wait until the following week to see him, I pulled out my phone and sent him a text:

> Hey! Do you have plans this weekend?

> Not yet 😊

> I was wondering if your unpacking skills were as good as your packing ones?

> Are you just using me for my physical capabilities? Lol

> No. I really want to see you. Unfortunately, I need to get some work done in my new place

> I'm just giving you a hard time. I'm happy to help

I chuckled at his message. If he only knew how much of a *hard time* he truly gave me. I'd jerked off more times in the last week than I think I had when I was a horny teenager.

> You want to come over around noon?

> I'll be there

At exactly noon, the concierge informed me that my guest was on his way up. The moment the bell rang, I swung the door open and pulled him inside.

Overcome with the need to kiss him, I pushed him against the wall and crashed my lips against his.

He pulled back slightly. "I thought I was supposed to help you unpack."

"That can wait. Right now, this is what I need." I kissed him again.

We stumbled over to the couch, where I laid down and pulled him on top of me. We quickly removed each other's shirts before I dove back in and continued to explore his mouth with my tongue.

When I spread my legs a little to make more room for him, I felt his erection press against my hip. My curiosity got the better of me, so I moved my hands between us and unbuttoned his jeans.

"Whatcha doin'?" he asked as he licked a path down my neck.

"I haven't touched you yet."

He lifted his head. "Is that what you want?"

"I really do." The couple of times we'd fooled around, he hadn't pushed for me to reciprocate in any way, but it was something I wanted to try.

"Then I'm all yours." He pushed his pants and boxers down his hips, his large cock springing free.

Reaching out, I traced my fingers up and down his length. After a few tentative touches, I grew a little bolder and wrapped my fingers around him. I marveled at the silkiness of him in my hand.

My own cock ached to get in on the action. I was going to ignore it so I could focus solely on Declan, but he pushed my sweats down and pulled me out. He gave my shaft a couple of pumps before he lined me up with himself and started rubbing our dicks together. I gasped because I hadn't ever felt anything as good as that before.

"Wrap your hand around both of us," he instructed.

My fingers couldn't circle all the way around both of us, but it didn't even matter when he started moving our hands up and down over us.

With the delicious friction our movements created, it took mere seconds for me to shoot my cum all over my stomach. Declan quickly followed with a groan, and I watched as his release mixed with mine.

"Now I'm not sure I'll have the energy to unpack," he teased.

"Well, let's get cleaned up. Then we can figure out what we want to do."

Once we both returned from the bathroom, I asked, "Did you have lunch yet?"

He shook his head. "I had a late breakfast, but I could eat."

"We can either order takeout, or I can heat up something I brought over that my chef put together."

"Do you even have any dishes to use?"

I nodded. "I unpacked a few things to get me by."

"Okay. We can have something here, but you don't need to eat what your chef makes when I'm around."

"Why's that?"

"Because I can cook."

I raised an eyebrow. "You can cook?"

"Don't sound so surprised. My mom worked long hours when I was growing up. Sometimes she brought food home from the diner, but if I was by myself, I had to make my own food."

My heart broke a little for the struggles he and his mom had endured after his dad died.

"Okay, let's see what you can whip up with what I have. Jasper brought over some groceries last night and I can replace whatever you use."

I pulled on my sweats, and then Declan followed me into the kitchen wearing only his boxers.

"Feel free to use whatever you can find in there." I pointed at the refrigerator and freezer. "Also, I've got a bunch of stuff in here." I opened the door to the walk-in pantry.

He rummaged around in the fridge, pulled out a package of chicken breasts and then found some frozen vegetables. "Do you have any rice?"

"Pretty sure I ordered some." Searching the shelves, I found the small bag. "Here you go," I said, handing it over.

"Thanks. Now where are your pots and pans? I also need a cutting board."

I dug through some boxes and eventually found the things he needed. While he started cutting the chicken into small chunks, I sat at the island.

"Don't you have some unpacking to do?" he asked with a chuckle.

"Yeah, but I'd rather watch you. You're pretty hot standing in my kitchen, practically naked."

He smiled. "Then sit there and enjoy the view."

"Oh, I will," I replied, knowing it was one I could easily get used to.

19

DECLAN

IT WASN'T THE FIRST TIME I'D WATCHED SEAN IN COURT, BUT IT WAS the first time I'd seen him command the courtroom while knowing what was under his suit.

Monday morning, I sat in the first row behind his table, my eyes fixated on him as he stood before everyone and argued his case. His hair was combed back and styled perfectly. Flashes of the way it hung in front of his eyes after we fooled around in his bed played in my mind. I tried to shake the thoughts of him naked from my head; I tried to focus on the way he carried himself with confidence as he presented his evidence, but I couldn't help the bulge in my slacks as I watched him in action.

As my gaze drifted down his body, the one I knew the contours of intimately, my mind filled with the way his strong arms wrapped around me and the taste of his lips against mine. Getting lost in those memories only made things worse because as Sean moved around the courtroom, I had to keep adjusting the position I was sitting in. No matter what I thought about, everything came back to the man in front of me and how he looked nude.

I longed to run my fingers through his short chest hair, to feel his body beneath my touch and lick my way over his six-pack abs. I couldn't wait to be alone with him again, to show him how much he turned me on just by being the man I admired. The man I had gotten to know beyond Ashford, Nolan & Torrance.

He was more than just my boss, and seeing him in his element only made me crave him more.

I HAD TO LEAVE THE COURTROOM BEFORE THE DAY WAS OVER BECAUSE I had another case to work on. It was for the best because, during lunch, I'd almost asked Sean for a nooner. It had been on the tip of my tongue, but since he needed to eat before returning to court—and because intercourse wasn't part of our relationship yet—I hadn't brought it up.

By the time I headed home, he hadn't come back to the office. I wasn't sure if he was planning to or not, but the court had been closed for a good hour, so maybe he went straight home. Since I hadn't heard from him, I shot him a text:

> Hey! On my way home. Hope the afternoon went well

I made it to the parking garage and slid into the SUV he had loaned me. It was weird to think I was driving his wife's vehicle, but I kept reminding myself he'd said it sat in his garage.

The shitty thing was: Betsy was sitting in a salvage yard because she needed a new engine I wasn't going to buy. The mechanic said it would be around three grand, and while I would essentially have that with my next paycheck, I wasn't ready to drop all my money on something that wasn't worth the cost. While Betsy had gotten me around for several years and helped me move to Boston, I knew it was time to let her go.

As I pulled out of the garage, my phone dinged with a text:

> Just having a drink with an old colleague. What are you doing for dinner?

I sent a reply when I stopped at a red light.

> Not sure yet. You?

> Jasper cooked something. Want to come over?

I put two and two together that Jasper was his personal chef, but did I want to come over? Hell yeah, I did. I'd been thinking about him naked all day, and there wasn't a chance in hell I would say no.

> Yes. When?

> I'll be there in 20

His new place was less than a two-minute drive and I went straight there and waited in the Escalade for him. Once I saw his Porsche pull in, I slid out. He was still dressed in the gray suit he'd worn to court, which didn't help my mind racing with lustful thoughts.

"Hey," he said as he climbed out of his car.

"Hey, yourself." I wanted to pull him to me and kiss him, but I refrained, knowing there were cameras around, and we hadn't talked about our relationship going public. If we even had a relationship. We hadn't discussed that either. We were still on the let's-see-where-this-goes train. "How'd the rest of today go?"

"Good. Winters will start his rebuttal tomorrow and then we'll have closing arguments." Sean loosened his teal tie as we walked into the building.

"How are you feeling about it?"

"We have a strong case." He pressed the button for the elevator.

"I don't doubt that. You were hot working that courtroom."

The doors slid open and we stepped inside.

Sean chuckled as he pressed the button for his floor. "Hot?"

I smirked as the doors started to shut. "I kept thinking about you naked."

"Oh, really?" He grinned.

I lifted a shoulder. "I couldn't help it."

"Well, now, when I see you in the gallery, I'm going to be wondering if you're thinking about me naked."

The elevator rose.

"The answer is 'yes'. Always yes."

Sean's smoldering gaze pierced my soul as he stared at me and licked his bottom lip. "I want to kiss you so fucking bad right now."

"Then do it," I challenged.

He groaned low and pushed me against the wall. I didn't resist as his mouth went for mine. We were all lips and tongues when the elevator stopped to let us out on his floor. I wasn't sure if he would stop, but he did and pulled me toward his condo. Once he unlocked it and we were inside, he pinned me against the closed door and went at my mouth again. I could feel his erection brushing mine as he pressed against me.

"Are you a top or bottom?" he asked against my lips.

I blinked and pulled back some. "A top or bottom?"

He looked into my eyes. "Yeah. I've been … researching."

"I usually bottom but—"

"Good. I want to fuck you."

I sucked in a breath. "Really?"

"You're not the only one who pictures the other one naked."

"Okay."

He grabbed my hand and led me to his bedroom.

"Have you ever done this before?" I asked, yanking off his tie as we stood next to his king-sized bed.

"Sex?" He cocked an eyebrow.

Dropping the silk from my fingers, I chuckled lightly. "Anal."

"Oh. Yeah, a few times."

"Good." I grinned and started undoing the buttons on his dress shirt. "Do you have lube and condoms?"

"Top drawer." He tilted his head toward the nightstand we were standing in front of.

"So, you're ready," I said with a wicked grin as I slid my hand down the front of his body to his cock still hidden by his trousers. He was hard beneath my touch. "Yep, you are."

"I think I've been ready since I jerked off the night of our first kiss and couldn't get you out of my head."

His affirmation surprised me. "You masturbated that night too?"

"I couldn't help it. I was so fucking hard thinking about your mouth."

I groaned and got to work on his pants. Once his belt was free, I unbuttoned his slacks and slid them down his legs. I followed, getting on my knees. When I looked up at his face, he shook his head.

"If you suck me off, I won't last."

"Damn, Bossman. Are you greedy for my ass or what?"

"You have no idea." He strode to the nightstand and pulled out the box of rubbers and a bottle of lube. "While I put on a condom, you get naked."

"Yes, sir." I grinned and quickly got to my feet.

As Sean stripped out of his pants and got ready, I removed my clothes and then leaned back on the bed, admiring his solid body. He was in even better shape than I was, and thinking about his hard length stretching me was making my dick leak.

"How do you want me?" I asked, watching as he coated his long shaft with lube.

"On all fours."

I didn't hesitate to flip over and get onto my hands and knees in the middle of the bed. He got onto the bed behind me, nudging his dick between my ass cheeks and making me moan.

"Damn. Hearing you moan just made me harder," he admitted. Leaning down, he placed kisses down my spine.

A shiver raced through me and I fisted my cock to give it a tug.

"Ready?" he whispered.

"Yes," I panted, sliding my hand slowly up and down my shaft.

Looking over my shoulder, I watched as he poured lube down my crack and then used his fingers to spread it around my hole. I hissed as he tentatively pushed the tip of his finger inside to prepare me.

"Do it," I urged, rocking my ass back toward him.

Sean slipped his finger inside, gave it a little swirl, and then slid back out before adding another finger to the mix. "You're so tight."

"Yeah, but I'm ready. I can't wait any longer." I continued to pump myself slowly, my cock already aching for release. I dropped my gaze to the bed and relished the feeling of him stretching me. "Please," I begged.

"Who's the greedy one now?" He removed his fingers and glided the crown of his cock through my crack.

"Me. I want to feel you deep inside of me, Sean," I moaned.

He groaned and pressed his tip against my puckered rim. Gradually, he filled me and I helped him go deeper, pushing my ass back against him.

"Fuck, you feel amazing."

"So do you." I stopped working myself and laid my head on the bed instead. I reached back with both arms and used my hands to spread my ass wider.

"Jesus," he breathed. "The sight of my dick sliding into your ass is enough to make me come."

"Not yet. You feel too good."

"I don't know, Dec. It's been a long time since I've fucked someone."

"Then let's come together."

With my head still on the bed, I reached for my dick again and stroked it in sync with Sean's thrusts. We were moaning and groaning, the bed was rocking, and our bodies were coated with a light sheen of sweat as we both raced to the finish line.

"Next time I want to watch you come," Sean panted, his hips still thrusting.

"Next time, I want to ride you."

My mind latched onto his words, and I began to overthink about Sean wanting to fuck me again. As a result, it didn't register at first when he pulled out of me.

"Actually, turn over," he ordered.

I flipped onto my back. He stepped off the bed, grabbed my legs, and dragged me to the side of the bed. I lifted my hips, eager for him to fill me again.

"Yeah, this is much better. I want to remember what your face looks like when I make you come so while I'm jerking off, I can think about you coming too."

"Jesus, Bossman. Didn't know you were such a dirty talker."

"Neither did I." He pushed into me again. "You've lit some sort of spark in me, and I know I'm going to be thinking about this moment until we do it again."

I fisted my cock once more. "Then make me come."

Sean leaned forward and took my mouth with his. We kissed like we were starving for each other, our tongues sloppy as they tangled together. He was fucking delicious, and the way he was fucking me, hitting the spot that made me see stars, was the icing on the cake.

"I'm going to come," he panted, breaking our lips apart.

I worked my dick faster, trying to catch up. "I'm right there," I groaned.

We locked eyes. After a few more thrusts, his body jolted as he came. I jerked faster and a moment later, I was spilling my seed onto my stomach and chest, my back arching and my eyes rolling into the back of my head.

He attacked my neck, kissing his way up to my mouth again, all while staying inside of me. We kissed for several long moments and when he pulled back, both of our chests were coated with my jizz.

"Looks like we need a shower." He winked.

AFTER GETTING CLEANED UP, SEAN AND I WENT TO HIS KITCHEN dressed only in our boxers. We were both starving because the shower led to another round and we'd worked up an appetite.

"All right, let's see what culinary masterpieces Jasper has prepared for me today," Sean said, swinging open the fridge door.

When I peered inside, my stomach growled. The shelves were stocked with neatly arranged containers.

"Looks like Chef Jasper has been busy," I remarked, a smile tugging at the corners of my lips.

Sean chuckled, plucking out a couple of containers and setting them on the counter. "Indeed, he has."

"I thought he was just making you food for tonight?"

"He tends to have several meals prepared for me because he has other clients."

"Oh, gotcha. So what did he make?"

Sean opened one container. It looked like it was mashed potatoes.

"It's cottage pie."

"I've never tried it before," I admitted.

"Really? What about shepard's pie?"

I shook my head. "I've heard of it but haven't had it."

Sean turned to the oven to preheat it as he spoke. "Shepard's pie is made with lamb, but I prefer ground beef, so this is cottage pie. There are some spices and peas, carrots, and sometimes corn topped with cheesy mashed potatoes. Once I heat it and the potatoes brown, it will warm your heart. Just watch."

"Can't wait."

While the oven heated up, Sean grabbed two wine glasses.

"Did Jasper unpack everything for the kitchen?" I asked. When I was over at his place on Saturday there was still a lot to be done, and now it appeared the kitchen was taken care of.

"I think so. I hated to make him unpack the stuff, but he was willing when I said he could organize everything the way he wanted."

I looked around the open floor plan and saw several more boxes in the living room still to unpack. "How long until the food is ready?"

Sean popped the cork on a bottle of red wine. "Twenty-five to thirty minutes once it's in the oven."

"Want me to help unpack more?"

"You don't need to do that."

I watched as he poured a glass of wine. "I know, but I want to. We didn't get that much done the other day."

"Are you sure?"

I shrugged. "Yeah, why not?"

"Okay." He placed the glass in front of me. "But just until dinner is ready. I don't want you to think that's the only reason I invited you over."

"Please." I chuckled and took a quick sip of the wine. "I'm sure I can think of other reasons."

"Behave." He swatted my ass playfully. "Or we aren't going to eat at all."

We walked more into the living room and I went to a box that was labeled: FAMILY PICTURES

"Start with any box?" I asked.

"Might as well. They all need to be unpacked."

I set my wine on the glass coffee table and used a box cutter nearby to cut open the tape. Sean's place had built-in bookshelves, so I walked over to it with a stack of picture frames while he opened another box.

As I was arranging the frames, one of the photos caught me off guard.

"Who's this?" I asked, pointing to a guy who looked familiar.

Sean came closer. "That's my son, Ryan. You probably remember him from Fallon's wedding."

I sucked in a small breath. I knew Ryan, and it wasn't from Fallon's wedding. "Your son?"

Sean arched a brow. "Yeah." He was probably wondering why I had a look of horror on my face. "Why?"

"I ... ah ... shit ..."

"What?"

I marched back to my wine and chugged it. "Okay, don't freak out."

I was the one freaking out but only because I wasn't sure how Sean was going to take the news.

"Spit it out, Dec."

"Okay." I took a deep breath. "A few years ago, I met Ryan at a club and we ... ah ... you know."

Sean blinked. "Had sex?"

I nodded, not able to find any more words.

"Oh ..." He walked over to the large window that overlooked the twinkling lights. "You had sex with my son and we just ..."

"Yep," I drew out the word. "But I didn't even know his name, and I made it clear I wasn't interested in more than a one-night stand."

Sean turned away from the window and I braced myself for his reaction. After a moment of tense silence, he let out a long sigh and ran a hand through his salt-and-pepper hair. "Well, shit," he muttered under his breath.

I winced, waiting for him to explode in anger or disappointment. Instead, he surprised me by letting out a short laugh and shaking his head.

"Of all the clubs in all the cities, my son had to walk into the one where you were?" he said, a wry smile on his lips.

I couldn't help but let out a nervous chuckle. "It was at Chrome, which is kinda the "it" place to go now."

"Well, I can't say I expected this little bombshell today, but I appreciate your honesty."

I moved to him and grabbed one of his hands. "I'm really sorry. I didn't know he was your son, and it was a long time ago. I promise it didn't mean anything."

He cupped my cheek. "Hey, it happened before us, and what's done is done."

"Thanks for not freaking out," I said sincerely. "I wouldn't want this to make you see me any differently."

He dropped his hand. "I don't think I will, but I do need to talk to Ryan."

"Of course. But just so you know, it was purely sex. What I feel for you is so much more."

He leaned in and brushed his lips over mine. "I feel the same way."

20

Sean

The Acosta trial consumed a majority of my time during the week. As much as I wanted to see Declan, I still needed the time to come to terms with everything that had happened when he'd come over on Monday.

I could not deny I'd enjoyed the sex. I could still remember how good it felt to be buried in his ass and the way his face looked when he came. But I was still trying to wrap my head around the idea that the first person I'd been intimate with in over five years was a man. And it was a guy who had previously hooked up with my son.

Although I'd been dismissive of Declan's revelation when he first told me, I wasn't entirely sure how I felt about it now that I'd given it more thought. When Morgan had mentioned I should sign up for The Click, I'd thought the idea of being on the same dating app as my kid was weird, but that didn't even come close to sleeping with the same person as Ryan had. The more I thought about it, the more concerned I became.

Declan had been adamant it had only been a random hook up and nothing more. But what if Ryan felt differently? It was something I needed to clarify with my son, yet I wasn't looking forward to having the conversation. Would I be able to give up whatever I had going on with Declan if Ryan had an issue with it?

Since the week was over and the case was in the hands of the jury, I wouldn't be able to avoid dealing with everything in my private life much longer.

As I pulled into the parking garage of my condo, my stomach dropped when I saw Ryan's gray Mercedes coupe. Instantly, I felt like an asshole for having a negative reaction to my son being at my place. It wasn't his fault I was twisted up in knots about recent developments.

Grabbing my briefcase, I made my way toward the elevator. The doors closed behind me, and while it ascended to the twenty-fourth floor, I attempted to figure out how I was going to approach the impending conversation with my son.

When the doors slid open, I took a deep breath and walked toward my front door and entered the code on the keypad. My mind was so focused on talking to him, it took a second for my brain to register what was happening in my living room.

Ryan was sitting on my white leather couch, while Jasper was kneeling on a throw pillow between his splayed legs. I spun around and bumped into the console table with my hip, causing it to slam into the wall.

"Fuck!" I rubbed the sore spot that was likely going to bruise.

"Holy shit!" Ryan shouted. "Aren't you supposed to still be at work?"

Keeping my back to them, I responded, "I came straight home after court instead of going to the office."

"Sean, I'm so sorry," Jasper pleaded.

I heard what sounded like the rustling of clothes, which was confirmed when Ryan said, "You can turn around now."

Slowly, I faced them again. Ryan was sitting on the couch while Jasper stood across from him and stared at the floor, refusing to look in my direction.

"That was completely unprofessional. I should go," he stated.

"Can't say I was expecting to walk in on that." I waved my hand toward the couch. "But you don't have to rush out of here."

"I already finished cooking. I'll make your plate and then be on my way." He scurried over to the kitchen.

My gaze drifted over to Ryan, and I quirked an eyebrow.

"What?" He chuckled quietly. "Like I said, I wasn't expecting you to come home this early."

Glancing at Jasper, who had his back to us, I lowered my voice and said, "I'm going to change, and then we should probably chat after he leaves."

"Am I in trouble?" he teased.

Rolling my eyes, I shook my head. "I'll be back."

Tossing my suit jacket on the chair in my bedroom, I glanced at the boxes that I still needed to unpack. With any luck, I could finish everything over the weekend unless Declan came over again.

I changed into a black T-shirt and jeans before returning to Ryan, who was sitting at the kitchen island, whispering with Jasper. They stopped talking when they saw me, and I took a seat next to my son.

Jasper turned and opened the oven. "I made salmon tonight." He placed a plate with the fish, brown rice, and asparagus in front of me, then grabbed some silverware and a napkin and set them beside the plate. "Would you like some wine as well?"

"That would be great," I replied.

He uncorked a bottle of pinot noir and filled a glass.

"You're not eating?" I asked Ryan.

"I had a late lunch with a client, so I'm not hungry, but I will take a glass of wine."

The room went silent as Jasper poured Ryan a glass and I began eating.

After a few minutes, Jasper was the first to break the awkward silence. "I'm going to head out. All of your meals for the weekend are in the fridge."

"Thank you." I wiped my mouth with my napkin. "I'll see you on Monday if I get home before you finish up."

A look of what appeared to be relief washed over his face. "Sounds good."

As soon as the door closed behind him, I shifted my focus to Ryan. "Why did he look relieved just now?"

"He thought you were going to fire him."

"Now I feel bad." I took a sip of my wine. "The thought never even crossed my mind, and I would have said something sooner if I'd known he was stressed about losing his job."

"So, you're not upset?"

"I didn't say that. You have your own place to do that kind of stuff. And you need to be careful if you're going to start something up with someone I've hired."

Ryan choked on the wine he just swallowed. "I'm not starting anything with him."

He was acting as though I hadn't just caught them in a compromising position. "What do you mean? I know what I walked in on."

"Just because we were messing around doesn't mean we're together or dating."

"Does Jasper know that?"

"Of course. I may not be interested in a relationship, but I'm not an asshole. I'm not going to hook up with someone without being upfront and honest with them."

"Have you ever been interested in someone long-term?"

The two of us had never talked about his relationships, or lack thereof before, but I needed to know for my own peace of mind.

He shrugged. "It's not like I'm against it or anything. I've just never met anyone who made me want to be a one-person sort of guy."

His words confirmed everything Declan had said when he explained what had happened between them, and that was a relief. I no longer had to worry that Ryan had wanted a relationship with the man I was developing feelings for.

"Are we done now with the uncomfortable father-son talk about my casual hook ups?"

I laughed. "Yeah. We're done."

While I'd been tempted to tell him about Declan, Ryan obviously didn't want to talk about his sex life any more than I did. Besides, Declan and I hadn't discussed our relationship, so telling my kids about him felt a little premature.

"So, did you just stop by to see Jasper, or was there another reason for your unexpected visit?" I flashed him a grin so he would know I was giving him a hard time.

"Actually, I'm meeting some friends nearby for happy hour, and then I'm going to hit up the clubs. I figured I could park in one of the guest spots here instead of trying to find parking in a public parking garage." He got up and put his glass in the dishwasher. "And since I'm here, I wanted to see if I could borrow Mom's Escalade?"

I swallowed the last bite of salmon and washed it down with my remaining wine. "Usually that wouldn't be a problem, but a friend of mine is borrowing it while his car is in the shop."

Ryan's brow furrowed. "Don't service centers usually have loaner cars for things like that?"

I lifted a shoulder. "He took it to a mechanic, actually," I explained, hoping he wouldn't ask any further questions.

"Well, do you think you'll get it back by Thanksgiving? I want to go skiing that weekend and was hoping to drive it up to the mountains."

When I told Declan he could borrow my SUV, I hadn't given him a timeframe for when I needed it back. And I wouldn't leave him without a vehicle just because Ryan wanted to go skiing.

"I'll ask him the next time I talk to him."

"Thanks, Dad." He checked the time on his phone. "Shoot, I gotta go. I'll see you later."

"Bye," I called out as he rushed out the door.

Later that night, I sat on my bed and used a pair of scissors to open a box filled with family mementos. Sitting inside, on top of everything else, was my wedding album. Like every other time I looked at the black leather-bound book, I was filled with happy memories of the times Melinda and I got to share for over twenty years, but that joy quickly mixed with sadness since her life had been cut far too short. With everything else going on in my life, I couldn't help but think back to a conversation she and I had shared shortly after she was placed in hospice care.

Melinda reached for my hand as I sat next to her bed. "*I want you to promise you'll try to find happiness again in whatever way you can.*"

I stroked the back of her hand with my thumb. "*Let's not talk about that right now.*"

It was hard enough knowing our time together was limited. I didn't feel like spending whatever precious moments we had left talking about my future without her.

"*You can't avoid it forever. And it will give me peace to know you aren't just going to throw yourself into work and forget how to enjoy life.*"

Of course, after so many years together, she knew that was exactly how I'd likely deal with my grief.

"*I hate thinking about any of that.*"

She gave me a small smile. "*I do too, but whether or not we talk about it, it's going to happen. So, can you please promise me?*"

I nodded. "*Okay, honey. I promise.*"

"Ah, Melinda," I spoke out loud, as I did occasionally, hoping she could hear me. "I lied to you when I made that promise. You worried I'd throw myself into work, and that's exactly what I did."

I opened the album and scanned the first photo. It was of us standing at the front of the church, holding each other's hands as we recited our vows.

"Things have changed, though." I let out a small laugh. "A lot. I've met someone who makes me smile again."

For some reason, saying those words to Melinda didn't feel weird. I had loved her wholeheartedly, and if things were different, we'd probably still be together. But that wasn't the hand life had dealt me. And I didn't feel like I was betraying her by pursuing a connection with someone new, because my happiness had been important to her.

"You'd probably be surprised to find out it's with a guy, though. Who would have seen that coming?" I flipped through a few more pages. "I definitely didn't. But I think a relationship with him could be good for me."

I finished looking at the pictures and set the album aside. Melinda would always have a place in my heart, but I also felt a sense of peace come over me after my confession to her. It was as if she had sent me a silent message telling me she was happy that I was finally embracing the life she wanted for me.

All that was left was telling Declan how I was feeling. I picked up my cell phone from my nightstand and sent him a message:

> Can you come over? I'd really like to talk

21

DECLAN

"Want to go grab a drink?" Camille asked when she stopped at my cubicle.

I glanced at the time to see it was after five and Sean once again hadn't returned to the office after court. I was a little disappointed because I missed him when he was away. It was strange because I'd never been so interested in a person before as I was in Sean Ashford.

Each morning, I looked forward to walking into the office and seeing him behind his desk. Well, I had always been excited to do that, but now it was different. It wasn't because I was a baby attorney and had to prove myself; it was because every shared look, every sly wink, every furtive roaming of our eyes over the other's body while no one was looking, felt like lighting a stick of dynamite that left me wanting to explode.

Explode down his throat.

Explode buried deep inside of him.

Explode while *he* was deep inside of *me*.

Even though Sean had never been with a guy before, it didn't feel as though he didn't know what he was doing. I often fantasized about locking his office door and doing it again while everyone in the office had no clue what was going on behind the closed door.

"Yeah, I'm just finishing up this discovery request," I replied to Camille. "Give me five and I can head out."

"Yay! My mother-in-law is in town and I'm dreading going home. I need a few drinks to relax and not be stressed when I walk in the door."

"In-laws are that bad?"

She lifted a shoulder. "Mine is. She thinks her son is still a child, and I feel like I'm walking on eggshells in my own house."

"Sounds horrible."

"You have no idea."

Camille walked away, presumably to get her things ready, and I quickly finished the document I was working on and saved it. It was ready for Sean's review, but since he wasn't in the office, there was nothing more I could do, and a drink did sound nice.

"Ready?" I asked as I stopped by Camille's desk.

"Yep." She stood and grabbed her purse.

We went to the elevators and took it down to the ground floor before walking outside. The fall air was turning crisp, and I pulled my coat tighter around myself. Thankfully, The Backyard wasn't that far down the street and, once inside, the warmth hit my cheeks. I shrugged out of my jacket and followed Camille to a high-top table in the bar section.

"So, is this a hard alcohol night or just beer?" I asked as we slid onto the chairs.

"Margaritas for me."

"Oh, plural." I chuckled.

"Yeah, I need more than one."

"Your mother-in-law is that bad?"

"Her intentions are good, but I can only handle so much."

"When does she leave?"

When the waitress came over, Camille ordered a margarita, and I ordered a Stella. Once the server left, Camille responded, "She doesn't leave for another week."

"Oh, damn."

"I know." She groaned. "She's been here a week already. Thankfully, I've been working most of the time."

Even though I had no clue what it was like to have an in-law, I'd seen movies and TV shows that depicted them to be horrible. I hoped the person I ended up with didn't feel that way about my mom. She was a saint, and when she called to check on me, she made sure to ask if I was taking care of myself. I knew she meant well.

"The only good thing," Camille continued, "is that my house is staying clean."

I barked out a small laugh. "That's a plus then."

"Yeah, I guess."

A few minutes later, the waitress returned with our drinks, and Camille and I didn't hesitate to take sips. Camille's was much longer than mine, though.

"All right. Enough about my mother-in-law. What's new with you?"

I'm fucking our boss. Well, fucked. Twice. Or he fucked me, really.
"Nothing much. Just the usual shit."

"How was your date on Monday?"

"It went well." I beamed, thinking about Sean and how it had been so much more than a date.

"Did you get lucky?" I cocked a brow and Camille went on. "Not to pry, but I'm not getting any while my husband's mom is here."

I chuckled. "Yeah, I got some."

"I'm jealous." We both took sips of our drinks. "I think Sean is getting some too."

I choked on my beer. "What?"

"He's like all smiley now, when before he was all about work and get me this and get me that and do this and do that. Now he doesn't even come back to the office after court."

So, I wasn't the only one to notice he wasn't returning from the courthouse.

"He did just move. Maybe he's busy unpacking or something," I suggested.

"Nope." Camille shook her head. "No one is that happy about moving and unpacking for weeks."

"True." I drank some more of my beer. "So, you think he's seeing someone?"

"Or at least dating again, and good for him. He's been single for years and after everything he went through with his late wife …"

"Yeah, I can't imagine."

Of course I wouldn't tell Camille I was the one Sean was seeing. I liked what he and I secretly shared, and I knew he had been hesitant to start anything with me to begin with. Whatever was happening between me and Sean, I was going to ride it as long as possible and not rock the boat.

And ride him.

"Anyway, I'm happy for him." Camille finished her drink with a big gulp.

"Me too."

She waved the waitress over and ordered another margarita. I was still nursing my beer. If Camille kept going, I had a feeling I was going to need to drive her home.

Two more margaritas for Camille, and burgers and fries for each of us later, Camille slid off her chair and placed her credit card down. "I need to go to the little girls' room and then head home."

"Sure." I watched as she swayed on her feet somewhat and headed for the restroom. My phone buzzed with a text, and I pulled it out of my slacks.

> Can you come over? I'd really like to talk

I let out a small groan as I read his words. He wanted to talk?

The waitress came over and grabbed Camille's credit card and I handed her mine as well. As she walked away, I replied to Sean:

> Talk? That doesn't sound good

> It's good. I promise

> Ok. I'm out with Camille now but can head over after

> I'll be waiting

Before I could text back and ask if he'd be naked, Camille returned.

"I think I need to order a rideshare," she stated.

"Three margaritas will do that to you."

The waitress returned and gave us the credit card slips to sign. After we did, Camille ordered a ride and we started for the front door. Her steps faltered a bit, and I reached out to hook my arm with hers.

"Are you going to be in trouble with your mother-in-law when you get home?" I teased.

"Probably, but I don't give a fuck."

I snorted a laugh. "Clearly."

"But thanks for having drinks with me. I really needed them."

"Anytime, girl. Just tell me when and where. I'm always down."

Once her car arrived, I got her inside, said my goodbye, and then headed for the parking garage where the Escalade was parked. As I neared, I sent Sean a text:

> Getting in the car now. Be there soon

> Good

AFTER PARKING IN SEAN'S GUEST SPOT, I HURRIED TO THE ELEVATOR and then up to his floor. I knocked and a few moments later, the door opened.

"Hi." I smiled.

"Hi." Sean grabbed my hand and tugged me into his condo. Once the door was closed, he pushed me against it and claimed my mouth with his. When we pulled apart, he asked, "Hungry?"

I shook my head. "Ate a burger with Camille."

"Okay. Can I get you a glass of wine or a beer?"

"Either is fine." I followed him toward the open kitchen.

He went to the fridge and pulled out two bottles of Stella Artois.

"Do you like this beer, or do you just have it for me?" I asked as he popped open the green bottle and handed it to me.

"It's not bad, but I got it because I know you like it."

"Thank you." I smiled warmly and took a sip. "But we can drink what you like too."

"It's fine." Sean waved me off. "But I wouldn't mind something stronger."

"Oh?" I cocked my head slightly.

"Walked in on Ryan and Jasper fooling around when I got home. Still can't get that image out of my head."

My eyes widened. "Seriously?"

He nodded. "Yeah. I didn't see anything other than the compromising position they were in, but still it wasn't something I really wanted to see."

"Maybe you just need to replace that image with one of your own," I suggested with a sly smirk.

Sean took a sip of beer and then set the bottle on the counter. He moved closer to me and then ran his finger down my chest. "I'd rather do more than what they were doing."

"So, does this mean you're okay with what we talked about last time?"

He met my stare. "About you and my son?"

I nodded. "Yeah. I wasn't sure if that would change things."

"He confirmed 'sex is just sex'."

"The sex with me?"

Sean shook his head. "I didn't mention you specifically."

"Oh. That's good."

"I'm not ready to tell my son—or anyone for that matter—what we're doing."

"Me either," I admitted. I wasn't ashamed of what we were doing, but I liked the sneaking around. Being sneaky made me feel things deep inside that made me giddy. If people found out about us, I didn't want them to think I was sleeping with the boss to get ahead, because that wasn't the case at all. Sean Ashford was drop-dead gorgeous, and I wanted to devour every inch of him every fucking day. Plus, I liked making him laugh. When he did, it made me happy.

"Good."

I was worried that bringing up Ryan had completely killed the sexy vibe we had just started until Sean leaned in and captured my mouth with his. The kiss lit a fire inside of me, and when he unbuckled my belt and led me to his bedroom, I knew of only one way to put out the flame.

We fell onto his big bed, our bodies tangled as our lips consumed each other. We ground against one another, our hands roaming over every inch we could reach. I could feel his cock hardening against mine as they rubbed together. A part of me wanted to hurry and strip our clothes off and have him sink into me, but another part wanted to relish the way he kissed me. The way he cupped my face and tried to bring his mouth closer than it could possibly get. The way he sucked my tongue and moved his lips against mine.

He reached for my tie to loosen it, but I said, "Kiss me more."

And he did, then turned me onto my back as he lay on top of me. His hips rolled into mine and we savored the moment, just kissing and humping. After a long day at the office, I knew I'd rather be right there, being consumed by this man, than anywhere else.

"You're so sexy," he breathed, breaking away from my lips for a moment.

"So are you," I replied and latched onto his neck.

My tongue ran up the side, tasting his salty skin. He moaned, and his hips ground harder into mine. As I licked and sucked, he worked on my tie. Once he had it free from my shirt, he unbuttoned my collar. We kissed again as he slipped each button through its hole, and as he worked his way down, he kissed my neck to my bare chest he had exposed along the way. I arched my back, moaning as each touch of his lips made my body hotter.

"I can't wait any longer," he admitted and rose to straddle my hips.

I gave a quick nod and reached for my belt, while he finished with the buttons on my shirt. He backed up so I could strip the shirt off my arms, and then we were both in a frenzy to get naked.

As soon as we were, I was salivating to taste him, to run my tongue over every inch of his body. But instead, I kissed him briefly and then said, "On your stomach."

He cocked a brow but then turned and lay face down on the bed. His firm ass begged to be touched, so I grabbed each cheek, squeezing them before getting a condom and the lube from the nightstand drawer.

Crawling on top of him, I kissed my way up his back until I got to his ear and whispered, "Now it's time for my dessert."

He groaned and lifted his ass slightly, as though he knew what I wanted.

And maybe he did.

Working my way back down, I kissed his back until I got to his perfect ass. I spread his cheeks apart and gave his hole a little swipe with my tongue. He moaned, raising his hips again as though to encourage me to keep going.

"You like that?" I asked.

"Yes," he breathed.

He panted and moaned, and his fists clenched the sheets as I twirled my tongue around his tight hole. I licked it like it was covered in icing and I had to get every drop. My dick ached for attention, so I reached down and stroked myself as I devoured him.

"I want your finger," he whimpered.

I grabbed the bottle of lube and squirted some onto my fingers. Sean stayed on his stomach as I ran my hand down his crack and then slid the tip of my finger into his tightness. He moaned and clenched the sheets again, so I went farther, going all the way to my first knuckle before withdrawing.

"Feel okay?" I asked, even though his reaction told me the answer.

"God, yes."

I went back in, this time going all the way in with my entire finger and giving it a few pumps. "You want another?"

Sean thought for a moment and then shook his head. "No. I want to be inside of you now."

The man didn't have to tell me twice. "Flip over then."

He rolled onto his back after I removed my fingers. While he sheathed himself with the latex, I grabbed the lube again and rubbed it onto my hole. Getting some more, I pressed a finger into my asshole to prepare for his big dick.

Once we were both ready, I poured more lube onto his hard length, gave it a few pumps, and then straddled his hips. I reached back and guided him to my opening and ever so slowly lowered onto his steel rod.

Leaning forward, I kissed his perfect lips. His hands went to my hips, and he held on as I rolled my pelvis until his cock slid past my tight rim. Sean reached down to grab my ass cheeks and spread them wider as he slipped in further.

"Fuck," I hissed, the burn temporary as his girth stretched me.

We locked eyes, and he gently rocked his hips, helping me as I sank onto him. Once he was in to the hilt, I started sliding up and down his dick in a rhythm that had us both panting and moaning. My shaft rubbed against his belly with the movement, and the added friction sent every nerve in my body into overdrive.

"That's it," he praised, and we both moved faster, his thrust meeting mine as I rocked my hips.

Covered with sweat, I bounced on him over and over as both of us got closer to falling apart. When I looked down at the man fucking me, I realized I'd never known what being with only one person truly meant. Sean knew exactly how to work my body, how to make me come faster than anyone I'd ever been with. While getting off quickly may have been shitty in the past because getting off too soon was a buzz kill, I knew our moment wasn't going to be the end. I knew there would be another round, another time for me to get off and feel the pleasure of my release, as well as another day or hour or minute for me to make him come too.

"Oh, my god. Fuck yeah," I moaned and leaned down, kissing him briefly because that was all I could do between each pant.

"I'm almost there," he said.

"Me too."

Sean grabbed my aching cock and he stroked it. As he did, I slid my hips up and down his shaft until we both came, the white ropes of my cum coating his stomach as his ass clenched and he released into the condom.

When I was spent, I collapsed on top of him and tried to catch my breath. "Best dessert ever."

A COUPLE OF WEEKS LATER, I WAS ON MY WAY TO MY MOM'S FOR Thanksgiving. I was surprised Sean was okay with me making the five-hour drive to Pennsylvania, but he was adamant about me keeping his Escalade, and I wasn't going to say no because I really liked the SUV.

Pulling into the trailer park where my mom lived, I parked in her tiny driveway and then slid out. She rushed outside her trailer and stopped.

"When did you get an Escalade?"

"I'm just borrowing it from my boss."

"Your boss? Why?"

I hugged my mom as I answered, "Betsy died."

"I'm surprised she lasted this long."

"Yeah."

"How'd you get your boss to lend you a car?" she asked as we walked to the back to grab my bag.

I hesitated for a moment. Since she was my mother and I hated to lie to her, I told her the truth. "Betsy died while I was at his house."

She blinked. "At his house?"

I swallowed and opened the back door. "We're ... dating."

"You're what?" she gasped.

I leaned against the vehicle, rubbing the back of my neck nervously. "It's kind of a thing. Sean and I have been seeing each other for a while now."

Her eyes widened, and she clutched her chest dramatically. "You're dating your boss?"

"Yeah, it was unexpected," I admitted, pulling my bag from the trunk. "But he's a great guy and I really like him."

"But he's your boss, Declan."

He was more than that to me. "I know, but it's not like I'm getting special treatment around the office. We have a rotation for who gets new cases to work on."

Mom nodded slowly, still trying to process the bombshell I had just dropped on her. "Well, as long as he treats you right, I guess that's the main thing."

I slung my bag over my shoulder. "Don't worry, he treats me *very* well."

22

Sean

Every year since Morgan was a little girl, she and Melinda had a tradition of going out shopping on Black Friday. It continued until Melinda got too sick to take her, and instead of letting the tradition end, I stepped in and began going with my daughter.

Dealing with crowds and the chaos that came with it wasn't my idea of a good time, but I was happy to follow my daughter through an endless stream of stores because doing it together meant a lot to her. However, we had been going for four hours, and I was tired.

"Do you have many more places you want to check out?"

"Just this one." She pointed at the makeup store across from us.

I noticed a jewelry store next door and nodded my head toward it. "I'm going to take a look in there. I'll come find you when I'm done."

"Okay," she replied as we headed in separate directions.

Entering the jewelry store, I walked over to a display case full of watches. There was a possibility I was moving too quickly, but I wanted to find something to give Declan as a Christmas present.

Christmas was my favorite holiday because I enjoyed selecting meaningful gifts for those I cared about. And that group of people now included Declan. What had started as more of a physical connection, had become more. He was smart and driven while also living life to the fullest. When I spent time with him, I was happier and more carefree. I hadn't felt that way in a long time, and I wanted to hold on to it for as long as possible.

"Hello, sir. Is there something I can help you find?" the sales associate asked as she stood on the other side of the counter.

"Could I see that one, please?" I pointed at a black and silver Rolex.

"Of course." She slid the glass case door open and placed the watch on top. "Is this for yourself or a gift?"

Even though Declan and I weren't telling anyone about our relationship, this woman didn't know me, and it was exciting to say the words out loud. "It's a gift for someone I'm seeing."

"You're seeing someone?" my daughter's voice shrieked.

I spun around. "You're done already?"

"They didn't have the eye shadow palette I wanted," she huffed. "But that doesn't matter. Why didn't you mention you were dating somebody?"

For a split second, I wondered if I could come up with a lie to avoid confirming what she'd overheard, but nothing came to mind. "It's new, and we haven't told anyone yet."

"Oh ..." Her gaze shifted to what I was holding, and her eyes widened. "Wait, that's a man's watch."

"Uh—"

"I'm going to give you a moment," the saleswoman said and moved across the store, keeping me in her sight, likely since I still held the Rolex.

"Dad, are you dating a guy?" Her tone suggested she was genuinely curious rather than upset.

I took a deep breath. "I am."

She smiled. "Well, are you going to tell me who he is?"

"He and I agreed to take things slow and keep our relationship between us for now."

Morgan arched an eyebrow. "You're taking things slow, but you're looking at expensive watches for him?"

"When we are both ready to tell people, you'll be the first to know."

"Fine." She pouted. "But I don't want to wait forever to meet him. You've always said my boyfriends needed your seal of approval, and now the tables have turned."

"Got it." I chuckled and waved the saleslady back over. Little did my daughter know she already knew who I was dating. "Now let me buy this, and then we'll get out of here."

DURING THE DRIVE BACK TO MY CONDO, MY PHONE RANG, AND RYAN'S name popped up on the display.

I pressed the answer button on my steering wheel. "Hi, Son."

"Hey, Dad. Are you still out shopping with Morgan, or did she already max out your credit cards?"

"Hilarious. Just for that, I'm not telling you what I found out today," Morgan taunted.

"Morgan!" I whipped my head in her direction.

"What's going on?" Ryan asked.

"Nothing," I replied at the same time as Morgan blurted out, "Dad has a boyfriend."

"What?" Ryan gasped. "Did you just say Dad has a boyfriend?"

"I sure did."

I glared at my daughter, and she rolled her eyes as if she knew I wasn't truly upset with her. Our family rarely kept things from each other, so I figured it was only a matter of time before my son found out too.

"Who is this guy?" Ryan asked.

"He won't tell me," Morgan whined. "Claims they're taking things slow."

"C'mon, Dad. You gotta let us meet him."

You already have.

I shook my head to stop thinking about the fact Ryan and I had been intimate with the same man. It wasn't so much that I had an issue with it; I just found it odd and preferred not to focus on that detail.

"You will eventually. We just need a little more time," I explained.

"Okay." He sighed. "I was just calling to let you know I won't make it to dinner on Monday. The guys and I extended our ski trip another day."

Despite not being able to borrow the Escalade, Ryan had still headed to the mountains right after Thanksgiving dinner for a weekend of skiing.

"We can reschedule," I said. "Have fun."

"Thanks, Dad. I'll talk to you later."

"Bye."

"Bye, Ryan. I'll let you know if I find out any more information," Morgan stated.

"Sounds good, Sis."

I shook my head and disconnected the call.

LATER THAT NIGHT, AS I LAY IN BED, I DECIDED TO LET DECLAN KNOW my kids had found out I was dating again. I considered calling him, but he was still in Pennsylvania visiting his mom, and I didn't want to pull him away from whatever he was doing, so I texted him instead:

> Hey! How's your visit going?

I didn't have to wait long for a response:

> It's been good. I've missed my mom a lot, so this trip was just what I needed

> That's great. I'm sure she's happy you're there

> She is. What have you been up to today?

> I went shopping with Morgan

I hit send and then typed out another message:

> She found out I'm dating someone

> She did? How?

> She overheard me talking to a saleswoman when I was picking out a Christmas gift for you. And then she told Ryan

The dots bounced on the screen for a second, and I hoped he wasn't getting ready to tell me he was upset about the situation.

> First, you don't need to buy me a present. Second, how did she take it?

> I know I didn't need to buy one. I wanted to. And Morgan seemed fine with it. She told Ryan too. I didn't tell them who, but they know I have a boyfriend

> Boyfriend, huh? 😊

Shit. We hadn't defined our relationship yet, so I didn't know if he was comfortable with me using that term.

> Sorry, I should have discussed what words we are using to describe our relationship before saying anything

> Don't apologize. Boyfriend is good.

> Then boyfriend it is. I miss you

> I miss you too

> When will you be home?

> Sunday night

> You should come over so I can show you just how much I missed you

> I'll let you know as soon as I'm back in town

And when he arrived back in Boston two days later, he came straight to my condo, where I proceeded to make good on my offer.

23

DECLAN

"Declan. Got a minute?"

I turned to see Sean peeking his head out the door of his office. "Sure." Scooting my desk chair back, I headed for his office. He was still in the doorway when I walked inside and then he shut the door behind us. I lifted an eyebrow as I stood next to his desk. "Am I in trouble?"

"Big trouble." He grinned.

"Oh, I like the sound of that."

He strode toward me, took my face in his hands, and kissed me. "Sorry. Been wanting to do that all day."

"I'm not complaining."

"What are you doing tonight?" He walked over to his desk.

I leaned forward and braced my arms on one of the chairs in front of him. "No plans. Why?"

"Want to go to dinner?"

"Go out to dinner?" I asked to clarify what he meant.

"Yeah."

"Are you asking me on a proper date?" I teased.

"I guess I am." He smiled.

"Then I'm not saying no."

"Good. I have to go to court this afternoon, but I can pick you up at your place at seven."

"I'll be ready." I beamed.

Sean took a seat at his desk, and I turned and left to go back to my cubicle. The rest of the afternoon seemed to drag on as I anticipated where we were going and what an actual date with him would be like.

When it was time to leave, I hadn't seen Sean in several hours, and it only heightened my excitement.

"Leaving already?" Camille asked, as I gathered my things.

"Yep."

"Another hot date?"

"You know it." I winked.

She grabbed her handbag. "Well, mind if we walk to the garage together? I'm heading out too."

"Of course not."

Once in the elevator, I pushed the button for the ground floor.

"Where do you keep meeting these guys to date? An app?"

"Nope." I shook my head. "This is the same guy as before."

"Does that mean you have a boyfriend?"

I smiled as wide as I could because yeah, I did. "It just became official over Thanksgiving."

The elevator dinged on the ground floor and the doors opened, letting us out.

"I'm so happy for you."

"Thanks." I couldn't get rid of the grin on my face as I thought about Sean and his dark brown eyes.

"Are you bringing him to the office holiday party?"

"I ... ah ..." I stammered as I opened the door that led to the parking garage. "Maybe?"

He would be there, of course, but I wasn't sure if he'd be there as my official date, or I suppose a *public* date.

"I would love to meet him."

"We're still new."

"I get it, but the holiday party is fun. He'd probably enjoy it." She lifted a shoulder.

"We'll see."

We walked toward our vehicles and mine was closest. "See you Monday."

"Wait." She blinked. "You drive an Escalade now?"

"Just a loner while I save up money to buy another car. Betsy died."

"Damn. I was going to say: promotion, a new man, and a new car? Things are looking up."

"Well, they are."

"I guess so. Have a good weekend." She waved and moved toward her car.

"You too."

I hopped into the SUV, drove home, and got ready for my date with Sean.

I NERVOUSLY CHECKED MY APPEARANCE IN THE MIRROR FOR WHAT FELT like the hundredth time, smoothing down the front of my dress shirt and running a hand through my hair. Having dinner in public with Sean felt different, I suppose because it was our first official date, since it wasn't as though we hadn't gone out to eat together before. It made me wonder if we were going to hold hands, kiss, dine by candlelight, or enjoy the activities that came at the end of dates.

My phone in my pocket buzzed with a text and I pulled it out.

> I'm outside

My heart skipped a beat as though I hadn't seen him earlier in the day. I quickly grabbed my keys and headed for the door. After locking up, I walked downstairs and outside. Sean's Porsche was idling at the curb and I hurried to slide inside.

"Hey," he said with a soft smile, his eyes lighting up as they took me in.

"Hey," I replied.

He leaned over and placed his lips on mine. "Ready?"

I nodded eagerly, feeling a surge of butterflies in my stomach as he pulled away from my building. "How was court this afternoon?"

"Good. Judge dismissed the Beckett case."

"Nice."

"Yep, so now I have the weekend free."

"Oh yeah? Are you going to do anything fun?"

"I don't know." He stopped at an intersection and turned his head toward me. "Do you have any plans?"

"Are you asking because you want to spend the weekend with me?"

"Yes," he replied without hesitation.

I looked down at my dress shirt and slacks. "I didn't bring clothes for the weekend."

"Will you need any?" he deadpanned as he pressed on the gas.

A slow smirk spread across my face. "Touché."

"But I can turn around if you want to run in and grab some things."

"Nope." I popped the P and shook my head. "I like the idea of being naked with you all weekend."

"Good." He winked. "I have an extra toothbrush and whatever else you may need."

"The only thing I'll need is your big dick."

Sean chuckled. "Is that all?"

"And water. Probably should drink water."

"I have water."

"Then I'm all set, Daddy."

The car swerved slightly, then he asked, "Daddy?"

I wrinkled my nose. "Yeah, that just doesn't work for us, does it?"

He shook his head. "Not since I have kids your age."

"Well, I needed to test it out. I've joked about calling you daddy before."

"You have?"

"Way before we got together. But yeah, it doesn't feel right."

"Glad we got that out of the way," he teased.

Once we arrived at the steakhouse, Sean pulled his car up to the valet. He handed his keys to the attendant, and we strolled inside. There was no hand holding, but I was okay with it. We were out in public on a date, and I was all for it.

"Reservation for Ashford," Sean told the hostess.

She checked the list and then grabbed two menus before saying, "Right this way."

Following her through the dimly lit restaurant, we walked toward a table for two and each took a seat.

"Your waiter will be right with you." The hostess placed the menus down in front of us.

I kept stealing glances at my boyfriend as we looked over the menus. If I hadn't been hungry *and* excited about our date, I would have suggested we get our food to go. Instead, once our waiter arrived, Sean ordered a bottle of pinot noir, and we each ordered a steak with mashed potatoes and creamed spinach to share.

"So, Camille asked me today if I'm bringing my boyfriend to the holiday party for work," I stated, then grabbed a piece of the bread the waiter had placed in the center of the table.

"She knows you have a boyfriend?"

"Yeah."

"And what did you say about the party?" He slid his knife through the butter.

I shrugged. "I said maybe."

He stuck the bread into his mouth and chewed. When he was done, he said, "I think the party will be too soon to come out to everyone."

"Okay," I simply replied. I wasn't going to push him to do something he wasn't ready to do. I completely understood his apprehension about going public, especially at work.

"You're okay with that?"

"I know dating a guy—your employee—is a lot for you, and I don't want anything to cause a rift between us. I like what we have."

"Even if it's a secret?"

"Will it always be?"

The waiter approached with our wine. After Sean gave his approval, the waiter filled our glasses and then walked away.

"No." I lifted a brow and Sean continued, "It won't always be a secret."

"Then when you're ready, I'm ready."

"Thank you. And maybe a part of me is since we're out to dinner together, but I'm not ready to hold a staff meeting about my dating life. My kids don't even know we're seeing each other."

"I know, and like I said, when you're ready, I'm ready."

"Okay."

The rest of dinner was effortless as we discussed work and upcoming plans for Christmas and the new year. Despite the weight of our conversation about keeping our relationship under wraps, our undeniable connection seemed to deepen over dinner, and I was looking forward to spending the weekend together.

As we finished our meal, Sean leaned in close. "I have a surprise for you."

My heart skipped a beat. "A surprise? What is it?"

He grinned. "You'll see."

He signaled for the waiter, who came over. Sean handed over his credit card, settled the bill, and then guided me out of the restaurant. As we waited for the valet to get his Porsche, we stood side by side. My pinky finger lightly brushed his hand, and he turned his head to me and smiled. I wanted to lean in and kiss him, but figured it would be too much. As we stared into each other's eyes, a male's voice called out, "Dad?"

Sean and I both turned to face the person and my eyes widened as Sean said, "Ryan? What are you doing here?"

"I was just walking by on my way to a bar to meet friends. What are you ..." He trailed off as he looked at me. "You look familiar."

I swallowed hard. "I ... ah ..."

Ryan cocked his head as though he was trying to place where he knew me from.

"Son, this is Declan."

"Wait. You were at Fallon's wedding. You two ... He works for you, right?"

Sean and I both nodded.

"Is this who you're dating?"

"Yes," Sean confirmed.

"Okay, but I swear I know you from somewhere else."

I glanced at Sean, not sure if I wanted the ground to open and swallow me whole or the valet to hit me with Sean's Porsche and put me out of my misery because I had no clue what to say to Ryan. Plus, it seemed he did not recognize me from sleeping together, which had to mean I wasn't any good, and that made the situation even worse.

But then Ryan's eyes became huge, and he breathed, "Oh shit."

I groaned and rubbed the back of my neck.

"Um ... Dad ..."

"I already know," Sean stated and slung his arm across my shoulders, bringing me against his side.

"You do?" Ryan balked.

"I told him," I said, low.

"Wait." Ryan crossed his arms and looked at his father. "You're dating someone I hooked up with?"

"What I have with Declan is much more than a one-night stand, Ryan."

"Let me get this straight. Not only are you seeing someone I slept with, but he's the friend of your best friend's son, and your employee."

"No." Sean shook his head. "He's just Declan, my boyfriend."

My heart swelled at his words, and I wanted more than anything to plant a big fat one on him, but I refrained.

Ryan stared at us for a few moments and then said, "Okay. Whatever makes you happy."

"He does," Sean stated.

The valet pulled up with the Porsche, and Ryan said, "All right. Well, I better go."

"If you want to discuss this further," Sean said, "come by the condo next week."

"All right." The two men hugged. "See ya."

Ryan walked away, and Sean grabbed the keys from the valet and handed him some cash. Once we were inside the car, I blew out a breath.

"That was awkward."

"So much for not coming out to people." He pulled away from the curb.

"Are you upset?"

"Not at all." He shook his head. "I mean, I would have liked to discuss things in a more private location than the sidewalk, but it's fine. He'll probably tell Morgan though, and then shit will really go down."

"Why do you think that?"

"Because she wanted to be the first to know."

"Ah. Well, now what?"

"Now for your surprise."

My eyes widened. "We're still doing whatever that is?"

"Absolutely."

Once we pulled up to a secluded spot overlooking the city skyline, the sparkling lights below stretched out like a sea of stars, and Sean turned off the engine.

"Are we going to make out?" I teased, but hoped that was the case.

Sean chuckled. "I thought we could have dessert under the stars."

"Dessert?"

He reached into the small back seat and grabbed a paper bag. "Jasper made us dessert. I hope you like carrot cake."

"I do." I nodded.

"Great."

Sean unpacked the cake and handed me a fork. The awkwardness about running into Ryan had lifted, and as we ate the homemade cake while looking out at the twinkling skyline, I couldn't think of a better way to end our first date.

24

Sean

The office holiday party was being held at a hotel in downtown Boston near our office building. Every year, we went all out for the event, and it was always a hit with the staff.

I stood with the other partners, listening to Luke gush to Eli about a case he'd just won. His wife, DeAnna, was beside him with a bored expression on her face as she listened to her husband talk about work. My gaze moved to the doors, where I anxiously awaited Declan's arrival. We had stuck to our plan to attend the party separately, but I couldn't wait to see him.

"Hi, Luke," Emily greeted in a sing-song voice as she joined our group. She turned and gave his wife a once over before saying, "DeAnna, it's so good to see you again."

"Hello, Emily," DeAnna replied. She looked her up and down, just as Emily had done to her. "Nice dress."

Emily smiled and swayed side to side, her red dress swishing around her hips. "Do you like it? It was a gift from someone *special*."

Luke choked on the sip of scotch he'd just taken.

I slapped him on the back and whispered, "You need to do something before Emily makes a scene." I excused myself and headed toward the bar where Camille and her husband, Dane, were hanging out.

"You two having a good time?" I asked as I approached them and shook Dane's hand.

"Not as much as I could be if I could hear what they were saying over there." Camille gestured toward the group I'd just left. "That looks all sorts of scandalous."

"You have no idea. It's definitely safer over here." I chuckled.

The bartender came over, and I ordered another whisky. Once I had my drink, I took a sip and turned around to observe Luke and the people around him. It was impossible to miss how uncomfortable everyone looked. It made me wonder if I needed to chat with him on Monday about how his actions could affect the firm. It felt hypocritical to say anything since I had my own thing going on with a subordinate. However, unlike Luke, I wasn't married.

"Hey, Declan's here." Camille nodded toward the doors.

My head turned toward the doors, and my breath caught as he entered the ballroom. He wore a slim-fitting black suit with a gray turtleneck underneath instead of a dress shirt and tie. His chestnut hair was gelled and styled perfectly to the side, and his jaw was covered with just the right amount of stubble, which begged me to run my lips over it.

He smiled brightly when his eyes met mine, and he made his way to us. "Bossman!" He shook my hand, but the gesture felt wrong. It left me wishing I could pull him into my arms and kiss him in front of everyone. One day, maybe I could, but the middle of the office holiday party wasn't the place for that sort of declaration. We didn't need to become a spectacle like Luke and Emily.

"I'm glad you could make it," I replied, taking another drink of the smooth alcohol.

"Declan, this is my husband," Camille interjected. "Dane, this is our newest attorney, Declan Rivers."

"Nice to meet you, Dane." Declan shook his hand. "Your wife is one of my favorite people around here."

"One of?" Camille gasped playfully.

"Fine. You're my favorite," Declan corrected and gave me a subtle wink.

Dane chuckled. "She's had nothing but great things to say about you too."

"So, where's this boyfriend of yours?" Camille asked, scanning the room as though she might have missed someone walking in with Declan. "I was looking forward to meeting him."

I threw back the rest of my drink, wondering how Declan was going to respond to our coworker.

Declan looked at me quickly but then said to Camille, "Yeah, I know. Unfortunately, he had his own work thing going on tonight."

"That's too bad. Maybe he can meet us during one of our happy hours soon." She frowned.

"Maybe." Declan shrugged. "Now I need to order a drink.

I placed my glass on the bar. "I should probably go make my rounds."

"Okay. Catch you later, Sean," Declan replied.

After talking to almost everyone in attendance, I was desperate to get back to my man. I looked around the ballroom and saw him talking to Eli and Brent from accounting. He glanced up as if he could sense me watching him, and our eyes locked.

"Help," he mouthed as Eli held Brent's attention.

I pulled my phone from my pocket and sent him a text:

> Meet me in the lobby

Once I hit send, I turned around to wait for him outside the ballroom. The second Declan walked through the doors, I pulled him into the utility closet I stood in front of.

"What are we doing in here?" He chuckled.

"I thought you wanted my help?" I nibbled at his ear and then kissed a path down his neck.

"You're right." He let out a breath. "Looks like I need to thank you for rescuing me."

He dropped to his knees and made quick work of my slacks. My head fell back against the door the moment he took me into his mouth. It was definitely the best holiday party I'd been to.

A week later, it was Christmas Eve, and I was spending it laying on the couch with Declan in my arms, the flames in the fireplace and the Christmas tree lights providing the only light in the room. I couldn't think of anything better. He'd barely made it through the door two hours earlier before I stripped him out of his clothes and had my way with him right there in the living room.

"Do you have to go home tonight, or can you stay here and leave in the morning?"

His mom was driving to Boston to spend Christmas Day with him, but I wasn't sure if he needed to get things ready ahead of her visit.

"I can stay." He trailed a hand up and down my stomach. "She's supposed to get in around eleven tomorrow and Sam will be there because her family is celebrating tonight. What time are Ryan and Morgan coming over?"

"I told them we were eating lunch at one, so they'll probably show up around noon or so."

"Okay. Do you want to exchange gifts now so we can sleep in?"

"Gifts? I wasn't expecting you to get me anything."

"What do you mean?" He pushed off the couch. "Did you really think I wouldn't get you a gift after you said you bought me one?"

I sat up. "I didn't tell you that to make you feel you had to get one for me. I enjoy giving gifts. It's kind of my thing."

"Noted." He grinned and walked to his duffle bag he'd dropped by the door.

While he rummaged through his stuff, I went over to the Christmas tree and grabbed the wrapped box I had for him. I sat back down on the couch, and he returned with a box covered in silver paper and a red gift bag. He dropped down beside me and handed over the wrapped present.

"Open this one first."

I made quick work of the paper and found a bottle of Macallan. "How'd you know this is my favorite whisky?"

"I didn't know it was your favorite, but I knew you liked it. You're not the only one who pays attention." He beamed. "It's what you were drinking when we were in Cape Cod."

That night at the Donnelleys' house was my first glimpse of the man Declan was outside of the office. And while my feelings hadn't been romantic then, I remembered how much I'd enjoyed his company and getting to know him better.

"So, you were watching me all the way back then?" I teased.

"Are you kidding? I've been watching you since my first Fourth of July party at the Donnelleys'. Of course, back then it was just because I thought you were hot. It's obviously turned into more since then."

It was on the tip of my tongue to tell him how much he meant to me, but something held me back. Not that I doubted my feelings for him, but we weren't publicly out as a couple. Until I could give him that, I didn't think I should make any big declarations.

"Well, it's a great gift. Thank you." I gave him a peck on the lips. "Now open mine."

"You don't want to see your other one first?"

I handed him the present wrapped in green paper with a white bow. "I can't wait any longer."

"Okay." He chuckled as he untied the ribbon and carefully removed the paper in one piece. His eyes widened when he saw the white box with the Rolex logo. "You didn't," he breathed.

I smiled. "Keep going."

He lifted the lid, revealing the green jewelry box, and flipped it open. "Sean, this is amazing." He ran a finger over the black and silver face. "But it's too much. I can't possibly accept this."

"Of course you can."

"Thank you," he whispered with a look of appreciation on his face. "I love it."

He slipped the watch on and admired it for a few moments, then handed me the other gift he'd brought. "This seems a bit silly now, but I hope you like it anyway."

"I'm sure I will." I dug through the gold tissue paper and reached inside to pull out black fabric. I barked out a laugh when I realized it was a pair of boxer briefs with words printed on the crotch that read, "I love your ...," and in place of the word cock was the image of a rooster. "These are great. I can't wait to wear them."

"And I'm looking forward to getting you out of them when you do." He winked.

I wrapped my hand around the back of his neck and brought him in close. What was meant to be a simple kiss turned into a full-blown make-out session that led to me taking him again on the couch.

THE FOLLOWING MORNING, DECLAN AND I SLEPT IN AS WE PLANNED. After we finally climbed out of bed and dressed, I made us coffee while he warmed up a pan of cinnamon rolls Jasper had made.

"I wish you could stay all day." I handed him a steaming mug of liquid caffeine. "If I'd planned better, I would have told Morgan that I was seeing you, and we could have invited your mom over and all had lunch together."

"Are you ready for Morgan to know?"

I shrugged. "Ryan already does, and I'd be surprised if he hasn't already spilled the beans. Besides, I'm tired of keeping us a secret from her."

Declan gave me a soft smile. "Maybe you can plan something soon."

The phone that was connected to the concierge desk rang, interrupting anything else I was going to say.

"Hello," I answered.

"Mr. Ashford, your son and daughter are on their way up."

When I first moved into this building, I put Ryan and Morgan on my approved visitor list so the attendants didn't have to get my permission to allow them up to my condo every time they came over. Suddenly, I worried it hadn't been the best idea.

"Thank you, Peter. Merry Christmas."

"Merry Christmas, sir."

I disconnected the call and glanced at Declan. "Looks like that meeting is going to happen sooner rather than later. Ryan and Morgan are on their way up."

As soon as the words left my mouth my door swung open, and they both exclaimed, "Merry Christmas!"

As they crossed the threshold, they both stopped in their tracks, their gazes landing on Declan.

"What are you doing here?" Morgan asked him.

"Uh …" He looked at me with a worried expression.

"Have a seat," I suggested. "And we can chat."

Ryan remained quiet and sat in one of the high-back chairs that flanked the couch. I wasn't worried about him because he already knew Declan and I were together. But Morgan seemed less than thrilled, which I found odd.

"I'm surprised I missed your beater down in the parking garage. That thing sticks out like a sore thumb," she said as she walked past me and Declan, her arms full of gifts. She placed them under the tree and took a seat opposite her brother.

"Morgan, there's no reason to be rude," I admonished.

"I'm not being rude, but why are you here on Christmas? Don't you work for my dad?" she sassed.

I had no idea why she was acting the way she was or what her problem was with Declan.

"Wait. Is he the *friend* who borrowed the Escalade?" Ryan asked.

I nodded.

"You let him borrow Mom's car?" Morgan shrieked.

I grimaced at Morgan's high-pitched tone. "He needed a vehicle."

"Maybe I should leave." Declan stood.

I got up too. "You don't have to."

I turned back to Morgan and noticed she was staring at Declan's arm. It took only a second for me to realize she was looking at the watch.

"He's who you bought the Rolex for?" I could see the moment she realized what that meant. "Are you fucking kidding me? He's the guy you're dating?"

"He is," I answered unabashedly. I wouldn't be made to feel bad for who I wanted to be in a relationship with.

"You know he's just dating you because you've got money, right?" she sneered.

"Excuse me?" Declan gritted out.

"C'mon, you've got 'gold digger' written all over you. You're just a poor kid from the middle-of-nowhere Pennsylvania who meets his rich, widower boss and takes advantage of the situation."

Declan turned to me, and I saw the hurt in his eyes. "You don't honestly believe that, do you?"

"Of course not, but—"

"You know what, I'm just gonna go."

"Wait!"

"Obviously you need to work things out with your kids. Besides, my mom is probably waiting for me."

As much as I didn't want him to go, I could understand why he wanted to.

"Let me walk you out."

He shook his head. "No. You should stay here and handle things with them." He rushed to my room and returned with his duffle bag slung across his shoulder a moment later.

"Oh gross," Morgan groaned, likely realizing he had spent the night with me.

I glared at her, but quickly turned back to Declan. "We'll talk later."

"Sure." He nodded once and hurried out the door.

"Morgan, what the hell was that? I can't believe you actually said those things to him. How did you even know where he's from?" I bellowed as I pulled at my hair.

"Faye mentioned it a few times. She was worried he was taking advantage of her brother, but clearly, Fallon was too smart to get wrapped up in all that."

"Just because his childhood wasn't like yours doesn't make him a gold digger. You're being unfair."

"Am I? Ryan, you've been awfully quiet. What do you think?"

"Well, I already knew they were together," he answered.

"You did?" she squawked. "Why didn't you say anything?"

Ryan shrugged. "I honestly didn't think it was that big of a deal. But now I can understand your concern."

"Seriously?" I gaped at my son.

"Morgan has a point, Dad. I'm guessing Declan was the one who made the first move. You need to ask yourself why a young gay guy would pursue something with an older man who never gave off gay or bisexual vibes before."

"I think you guys are wrong about him. He's never given me a reason to question his motives."

"Give it some time. I'm sure he will, eventually." Morgan glanced at her brother. "I'm gonna go. Do you want to go with me or order a rideshare later?"

"You're leaving?" I asked.

She rolled her eyes. "I'm not feeling very festive anymore."

"I wish you'd stay," I muttered.

Ignoring me, she addressed Ryan again. "Well?"

He looked at me. "We rode over together. Maybe it's best if I go with her."

Morgan stomped to the door, not waiting to see if he would follow.

"Okay." There wasn't really anything else to say. The holiday had already been ruined, and it was probably a good idea if everyone took some time to cool off. "I'll call you later."

Ryan nodded, and then they left.

Later that evening, I still hadn't heard from my kids, so I texted Morgan:

> I hope you're okay. Can we talk soon?

Twenty minutes later, I'd still gotten no response from her and decided I should check in with Ryan:

> Hey! I texted your sister, but haven't heard back. How was she after you left?

Thankfully, I didn't have to wait long for his reply:

> She was pretty upset. I think she needs time to cool off before you guys talk things out

> What about you?

> I'm not upset. I just want you to be careful. I don't know what Declan's intentions are, and I don't want you to get hurt. But I also understand you can make your own decisions

> I trust him, but I don't know how to make a relationship with him work if you guys don't

> Maybe you need some time to think about things too

Maybe he was right. It felt as though I was in the middle, and I didn't want to be forced to pick sides. Deep down, I knew Declan was with me for the right reasons, and a part of me believed that was all that should matter. But the idea that my relationship with him could drive a wedge between me and my kids broke my heart. We had been through a lot as a family, and the one thing that had gotten us through the hard times was supporting each other. I didn't want to lose them now.

> Yeah, you're probably right. Can we get together soon though? I feel bad that Christmas was ruined

> I'd like that

After I stopped texting with Ryan, I couldn't stop thinking about

Declan. I hadn't heard from him, but I wasn't surprised. He'd been upset when he left, and who could blame him? It had to have been humiliating to have those accusations thrown at him.

Wanting to check on him and apologize for how things had gone, I sent him a text.

25

DECLAN

I TRUDGED UP THE STAIRS TO MY APARTMENT, MY MIND STILL REELING from the confrontation at Sean's condo. I fought back tears because I couldn't shake the feeling he was going to end things with me. Why would he want to be with someone his children didn't like or trust? I never once did or said anything that would lead anyone to believe I was after his money because that was so far from reality and had never crossed my mind. Yet, that was what they wanted to believe.

Unlocking the door, I pushed it open and was greeted by the smells of my mother's cooking. Every year, she'd arrive and get straight to making Christmas dinner of cornbread stuffing, green beans, mashed potatoes, and ham. Sadly, the thought of eating it made me sick to my stomach, and I knew it wasn't because of her actual cooking—which was delicious—but because of the turmoil playing over and over in my head.

Mom and Sam were sitting on the couch, nestled under cozy blankets, and watching a Christmas movie. As soon as they saw me, a look of concern graced their faces.

"Declan, what's wrong?" Mom asked as she stood.

"Hi, Mom." We engulfed each other in a hug. How did I explain what went down? I hated that this was how we were seeing each other after several weeks, but I couldn't have predicted how the morning was going to go.

"Did something happen with Sean?" Sam asked.

I nodded as I stepped back from my mom. "His kids freaked out about us dating."

"Oh, honey, what did they say?" Mom squeezed my hand.

Taking a deep breath, I plopped on the couch next to Sam. "They accused me of dating him just for his money."

Sam's jaw dropped, and her eyes went wide. "That's ridiculous! You've never mentioned his money. Ever."

I nodded. "I know, but since I'm driving his Escalade and I'm younger, they assumed I'm a gold digger. Plus, he got me this for Christmas." I pulled back my sleeve to reveal the watch on my wrist.

Sam gasped. "He got you a Rolex? Isn't that like ten thousand dollars?"

"How do you know how much it costs?" I questioned.

"Ballpark, but damn." She inspected it closely.

"You didn't ask him to buy you this watch, did you?" Mom asked.

I shook my head. "Of course not, but it's one more reason for them to think I just want his money."

Mom sat on my other side and wrapped her arms around me, pulling me into a comforting hug. "Don't listen to them. You know what's in your heart."

The accusations still stung because how would Sean and I ever be okay if his kids didn't approve?

"They just don't understand," I murmured.

"It sounds to me like they want his money and are afraid you're going to take it instead," Sam stated.

"It would be theirs to take," I said. "But no matter what, I'm not sure they'll ever trust me, and what if Sean believes them?"

Mom patted my knee. "If you're meant to be together, then you two will overcome this."

"And if we're not?"

"Then he isn't the one." Mom glanced at the beautifully wrapped presents under the tree, a warm smile tugging at her lips. "But how about something that will cheer you up? Are you ready to open presents?"

"Yeah, sure." I forced a smile as I watched Mom stand and move toward the tree in the corner of the living room. She'd made the trip to see me for Christmas, so the least I could do would be to make her holiday a good one.

And that was what happened. We opened presents, ate the delicious food she prepared, and fired up another Christmas movie.

Later that evening, as I was getting out of the shower, my phone dinged with a text:

> Sorry about today. I hope you're doing okay. I'm not sure what to make of everything and I just need some time. Hope you understand

I stared at the text, not sure what to make of it. Was it a breakup text or did he still want to see me while he figured things out?

My hands slightly shook as I texted back:

> Time away from me?

> It's not exactly what I want but I need to consider my children and their feelings

> Yeah but what they said isn't true. I don't want your money

> I know that

> Do you?

After I hit send, I wanted to take it back. I knew it was coming off like I was snapping at him, but I couldn't help it. The entire situation still stung.

> I do

> But with everything, like I said, I just need some time to think

> Good thing we aren't in the office for a week then

I hated how I was coming across, but I was still angry about the situation.

> I wouldn't say it's a good thing, but it gives me some time

> What about the Escalade?

> Keep it for now

> Are you sure?

> It would just sit in the garage and you need it

> I've been saving money. I can go get a new car

> It's fine

> Ok. Thanks. Enjoy the rest of your holiday. I'll see you back in the office after the first of the year

I left the bathroom and went to the living room where I was sleeping while my mom was in town. She and Sam were already asleep, and after silencing my phone, I passed out.

Merry fucking Christmas to me.

True to his word, I hadn't heard from Sean in days, and my mood hadn't improved. I tried my best to act happy in front of my mom and even took her around town and ice skating before she returned to Pennsylvania, but nothing I did made me forget about Sean

Ashford. I didn't think he'd fire me over the situation, but having to see him in the office everyday was going to be tough. I supposed that was one reason people shouldn't date their boss.

Lying in bed, I heard my phone ding with a text. I grabbed it and saw a message from Fallon:

> I'll be there in 20

I quickly typed back:

> Why?

> What do you mean why? NYE

I blinked and quickly looked at the date on my phone, not realizing it was the last day of the year.

> I'm going to bail

> Why?

> Not feeling it

> Are you sick?

> No

> I've never known you to turn down going out to party. Especially on NYE. What's going on?

> Just ... shit

> I'll be there soon and we can chat about it

> You don't need to do that

> I'm already on my way

I knew I wouldn't be able to stop Fallon from showing up, and it was my fault for bailing on him, but I really didn't feel like going out dancing. Drinking, maybe. Yeah, definitely drinking.

I quickly showered. As I left the bathroom to get dressed, there was a knock on the door. "Coming!" I called out.

"Not yet, you're not," Fallon teased from the other side. "Save that for someone else."

Wearing only a towel around my waist, I swung the door open. "Okay, maybe you were."

I rolled my eyes. "Just got out of the shower."

I let Rhett come inside and do his Secret Service thing as me and Fallon continued to chat at the door. I didn't even care that I was practically naked.

"Did you change your mind about coming out with us?" Fallon asked.

I nodded and leaned against the doorjamb. "I did."

"Good. Go get dressed and let's head out."

"This is what I'm wearing," I deadpanned, as Rhett gave the all-clear for Fallon to come into my apartment.

Fallon raised an eyebrow, scanning me from head to toe, and chuckled as he walked inside. "Yeah, okay."

I shrugged, a weak grin forming. "What? You think it's too formal?"

He shook his head and laughed. "Nah, but you're going to freeze your balls off."

"That's okay. I don't need them anymore." I shut the door.

"What the hell?" Rhett responded with a snort.

"Yeah, what the fuck are you talking about?" Fallon inquired.

I sighed. "It's Sean."

Fallon blinked. "What happened?"

I hesitated for a moment and then answered, "His kids accused me of only being with him for his money, which is absolutely not true."

"Wow, yeah, I don't peg you as someone after his money, but let's talk about that other part. You and Uncle Sean are together?"

I nodded once. "Yeah. Or at least, we were. But now I don't know. He said he needs time to think, to consider his kids' feelings."

"Damn, dude. How are you feeling?"

I lifted a shoulder. "I've never *dated* someone before, and I truly enjoy being with him. I loved everything about him, but now I feel as though I'm lost. I can't even enjoy New Year's Eve because all I want to do is stay home and think about him."

Fallon and his husband shared a look.

"What?" I asked.

"You're in love, my friend," Fallon answered. "You actually just said it yourself."

I cared about Sean a lot. I loved spending time with him at work and away from the office. Loved having our dinners at home together and carrot cake under the stars.

Hell, Fallon was right; I fucking loved Sean. My heart felt as though it was slowly shattering in my chest. All I wanted was to go up to Sean and have him wrap me in his arms and tell me everything was going to work out. That everything would be okay.

"Yeah, I do." I looked down at the carpet.

"Then this is what you're going to do."

My leg bounced up and down as the Secret Service vehicle pulled up to the curb in front of Sean's condo.

"What if he's not here?" I asked.

"He's home," Fallon stated.

"How do you know?"

Fallon gave me a I-fucking-know look but then asked Rhett, "Handsome, he's home, right?"

"Yes," Rhett confirmed.

"Alone?" I asked.

"We didn't get that intel," Rhett stated.

My eyes widened as I glanced at Fallon. The light in the vehicle came from the streetlights outside, so I could barely see his face. "What if he's not alone?"

"There's only one way to find out."

What Fallon had suggested I do sounded good before we got to

Sean's place. Now every nerve in my body was running wild, and I wasn't sure if I was doing the right thing.

If Sean would even want to see me.

"Sorry about ruining your New Year's Eve," I said to my friend.

"It's all good. I'm sure these boys appreciate not having to be on high alert in a nightclub," he responded.

"All right. Here I go." I took a deep breath. My heart pounded against my rib cage like it was trying to escape and possibly save me from the pain of what was about to come. But there was no turning back. If I went up there and told Sean what I needed to say and he turned me away, at least I would know. And they say knowing is half the battle. I was done being at war with my own thoughts and just needed answers.

Fallon gave me an encouraging nod, and I slid out of the SUV.

"If I'm not back in ten, take that as a good sign."

"Good luck," the guys called out, and I shut the door.

After walking into the building, I said hello to Peter at the desk and took the elevator to Sean's floor. With a shaky hand, I reached out and knocked.

Seconds felt like hours as I waited, my mind racing through a thousand different scenarios. What if Sean opened the door and slammed it shut in my face? What if he was with someone else? What if Morgan and Ryan were with him? What if he didn't love me back? What if he saw me through the peephole and didn't open the door at all?

However, the door opened, and he stood before me with a surprised look etched across his face. He was in a white T-shirt and gray sweatpants, and he'd never looked so damn handsome.

"What are you doing here?" he asked.

I swallowed hard, gathering every ounce of courage I had left, and met his gaze. "When I imagine ringing in the new year, you're the only person I want to share it with. You're the only one I want to kiss at midnight. I can't stop thinking about you. Every moment we shared. Every kiss. Every stolen glance in the office. And I know things have been complicated, especially with your kids, but I want you to know that my feelings for you are real." I took a deep breath and then went for it. "I love you, Sean Ashford. Like head over heels, so fucking in love with you—"

In one swift move, he took my face in his hands and silenced me with his mouth. Even though I knew I'd missed him, I hadn't realized how much. But at that moment, everything disappeared except him and me and his lips on mine.

When we pulled apart, he grabbed my hand and led me into his condo. He took me to his couch, and we sat facing each other. I wasn't sure what was about to happen. He glanced at the clock on the wall.

"We only have about thirty seconds, but I want you to know that you telling me you love me was exactly what I wanted to hear." As the clock ticked down to midnight, he leaned in, his eyes ablaze with love, and confessed the words that started to glue my heart back together. "I love you too, Declan. More than I ever thought would be possible again. You've brought light back into my life, and I never want to let you go. Things might not always be easy, and I've had my fair share of hard times, but I don't want to conquer those challenges with anyone but you."

The clock struck midnight, and we sealed our declarations of love with another kiss. As fireworks exploded over the river in the distance, I was hopeful we were going to make things work no matter what.

Our kiss deepened and before I knew it, our clothes were being tossed on the floor and we shared what had to be the best way to ring in the new year.

26

Sean

In the few weeks since the new year started, my workload had required a lot of late nights in the office, and this one was no exception. I was exhausted but still had a couple more things to finish before I could leave.

As I replied to a client's email, my phone began playing "Hail to the Chief," the special ringtone I'd assigned to Patrick Donnelley.

"Mr. President," I answered teasingly.

"Hey, Sean. How's it going?"

"Same old stuff," I replied. "Just busy with work. How about you? Staying busy leading the free world?"

He chuckled. "Pretty much."

When Patrick was elected president two years ago, I wasn't sure if it would change our friendship. But he was the same guy I'd met over twenty-five years prior, only he had a lot more responsibility than back then.

"So, I was calling to let you know Mary and I will be in Boston this weekend, and we were hoping you could join us for our family dinner on Saturday."

"Oh. I'd love to see you both, but I have plans on Saturday evening."

Declan and I had reservations for dinner at a new Italian restaurant that we wanted to check out. As much as I missed my friends, I needed to show him that he held a special place in my life, and I wouldn't bail on him just because other things came up, especially because things hadn't been fixed yet with my kids. I never wanted to give him a reason to doubt his importance to me.

"That's too bad. Is it a boring work thing?"

Until recently, the only thing that would have kept me from meeting Patrick when he was in town would have been work. I could have agreed and said that was the reason, but I was tired of keeping secrets.

"Actually, I have a date."

"Hold on a second. Are you serious?" He sounded more excited for me than surprised I was dating.

"I am."

"That's great news. Why don't you bring her over so Mary and I can meet her?"

"Uh ... there might be a slight problem with that."

"Why?"

I took a deep breath. I hadn't expected to drop this bombshell on my best friend over the phone, but I went with it. "Because there is no woman for you to meet. I'm ... dating a guy."

There was a beat of silence, and then Patrick said, "Huh, I didn't see that coming. But the offer still stands. We would love to meet whomever you're seeing."

I was about to tell him he already knew my boyfriend, but before I could, he said, "Sean, duty calls, so I need to go. I'll talk to you later."

"All right. Bye." I disconnected the call.

I pushed back from my desk and walked over to my door. "Hey, Declan. Can you come here for a minute?"

"Be right there, Bossman," he called out.

I went back to my chair and sat while I waited.

"What's up?" he asked when he stepped inside.

"Close the door."

He did as I instructed and then sat in the chair across from me. "Now I'm worried. You usually only call me in here to push me against the wall and kiss me." His voice had a hint of humor, but I could also hear a small amount of concern.

"It's nothing bad. At least, I don't think so. I just didn't want to risk anyone overhearing in case we aren't alone."

"Okay."

"Patrick Donnelley invited me to have dinner with him and Mary on Saturday."

"Oh." Declan nodded. "Do you want to reschedule our reservation?"

"No, I still want to go out with you on Saturday, but how would you feel about having dinner with my friends instead?"

His eyes widened. "You want me to have dinner with you and the Donnelleys?"

I nodded.

"As your boyfriend?" he clarified.

"I do, but only if you're comfortable with it."

"That's a big shift from you wanting to keep our relationship a secret."

Standing, I rounded my desk and knelt beside him. "I know, but ever since New Year's Eve, I've been thinking …"

"About what?" he prodded when I didn't continue.

"About how I don't want to hide you away when I love you so much."

Declan smiled brightly. "I don't want to hide anymore either."

"You don't?"

"I know we still have to figure out work stuff, and it has been fun sneaking around. But I like the idea of everyone knowing we're together."

"Me too." I pulled him toward me and pressed my lips to his. "Now

I just need to figure out how to tell them I'm bringing their son's friend as my date."

He laughed. "Good luck with that."

DECLAN AND I WERE ON OUR WAY TO THE DONNELLEYS' ESTATE IN Weston. Their place wasn't too far from my former house, but I hadn't been in the area since I'd moved a few months before.

"Did you get a chance to talk to Patrick yesterday?" Declan asked.

I shook my head. "I tried to call him, but he was in meetings all day."

"Guess it's not always easy to get a hold of the president."

"Nope. I usually only talk to him when he calls me."

"So, we're just going to show up and say 'surprise'?"

I took the exit toward their house. "Looks that way."

"Okay," he mumbled.

I glanced in his direction, and he was looking out the window. Lacing my fingers with his, I asked, "Everything all right?"

He shrugged. "I'm just worried. What if they react in the same way as Morgan?"

I squeezed his hand. "That's unlikely. They already know you, and you've been a guest in their home. If they had any problems with you, they wouldn't have let you spend the weekend in Cape Cod."

"Yeah, but I've only stayed with them as their son's friend, not the boyfriend of their closest friend."

"Patrick and Mary might be surprised when I tell them, but I don't think they're going to freak out."

At least I hoped they wouldn't. My friends were the best people I knew, but sometimes those people you thought you knew well could surprise you with their reactions to things. Like my daughter.

"That's all we can hope for, I guess."

We turned off the road and checked in with the Secret Service agents posted at the entry gate of their property. Thankfully, Declan had been previously cleared by the agency so there wasn't an issue of him being with me. Once they reviewed our identification and inspected our vehicle, we were waved through. I followed the winding driveway and parked in front of their whitewashed brick home.

"You ready?" I asked.

Declan nodded. "Let's do this."

We climbed out of my Porsche and made our way to the front door. Before we could knock, Fallon swung it open and stepped out onto the porch.

"Hey!" He gave us each a quick hug with the standard bro back slap. "My parents are in there talking about how excited they are to meet your new boyfriend. I can't believe you two are about to spring your relationship on my parents without warning."

"Do you think they're going to be upset?" Declan asked my nephew.

"Surprised? For sure." Fallon chuckled. "Upset? I don't think so. That's not the kind of people they are."

Declan let out a breath.

"See?" I rubbed the back of his neck. "I told you not to worry."

He tilted his head up, and I kissed him softly.

"Okay. I'm cool with you two, but I don't want to see my uncle and my friend kissing."

We all laughed, and I grabbed Declan's hand again. "Let's go inside."

"Mom, Dad, Uncle Sean is here with his boyfriend," Fallon called out as we followed behind him.

"You're ridiculous." I laughed.

Mary and Patrick rounded the corner with Rhett behind them a few seconds later.

"We've been looking forward to meeting your ..." Mary's words died off as she noticed Declan's hand in mine.

"Oh," she said as she turned to her husband. "I guess we've already met Sean's boyfriend."

Patrick quirked an eyebrow. "You two are dating?"

"We are," I answered confidently, pulling Declan closer to me. I wouldn't allow anyone, even the president of the United States, to make Declan ever feel insecure in our relationship again. After what happened on Christmas, he needed to know I was proud to have him by my side.

"Wow." Patrick chuckled. "Definitely wasn't expecting that, but congratulations."

"I'm so happy for you both." Mary smiled brightly.

"Thank you." I kissed Declan's cheek.

"Let's go have a drink in the living room," Patrick suggested. "Dinner should be ready in about an hour."

Fallon grabbed a few beers for Declan, Rhett, and himself, while Patrick poured a glass of wine for Mary and Macallan for us. Declan looked at the drink in my hand and winked, reminding me he'd known Macallan was my favorite whisky because I drank it with Patrick.

The conversation among the six of us flowed naturally, and it was a relief that my friends were accepting and continued to treat Declan the same as they always had.

Unfortunately, as soon as I started to relax, I heard the front door open, and the familiar voices of Morgan and Faye carried over to us.

"Shit," I grumbled under my breath, but Declan must have heard me because this time, he offered his hand in support.

"Girls, come join us," Mary called out.

The minute they walked into the living room, Morgan's eyes found Declan, and then she turned to me. "I can't believe you brought him here." It was the first words she'd spoken to me in weeks.

"Morgan, stop."

My daughter rolled her eyes. "I can't believe you're still dating someone who is using you for your money."

"Can we not do this here?" I implored.

"Why not? I'm sure Patrick and Mary don't want you being taken advantage of," she argued.

Patrick's brow furrowed. "Morgan, I don't know why you think Declan has ulterior motives—"

"I'm sure Fallon told you about Declan's background, because Faye knows all about it."

Declan's head whipped over to Fallon. "What is she talking about?"

It was Faye who responded, "My brother told me about you being some trailer park kid attending Hawkins Law on a scholarship because you couldn't afford it on your own. Hell, you could barely pay for your drink at Fallon's bachelor party."

"Faye!" Fallon shouted. "You're making it sound like something bad. All I ever said was how much I admired Declan because of how hard he had to work to make his dreams of attending law school a reality. I was in awe of him, not judging him."

"I gotta say, I'm disappointed in you, Faye," Patrick stated. "We didn't raise you to act like this or to look down on people who didn't have the same advantages as you."

"Morgan, you owe Declan an apology," I added. "He's the person I want to be with, and your accusations aren't going to change that."

"But—"

"No. I love him, and you need to figure out how to accept that." It killed me to take such a hard stance with her, but Declan didn't deserve to be disrespected.

"Well, I can't do that." Morgan turned to her friend. "Let's go."

The two of them spun around and headed for the door. As soon as we heard it slam behind them, everyone began speaking at once.

I wrapped my arm around Declan and kissed his temple. "I'm so sorry. I can't believe how horrible Morgan is still acting toward you. Are you okay?"

He nodded. "It sucks having her toss out those accusations again, but I'm fine. What about you?"

I shrugged. "I'll be all right. It's just a shitty situation."

"Declan, I don't even know what to say." Mary looked horrified by what had just happened. "Faye was out of line, plain and simple."

"Please know we don't share our daughter's opinion," Patrick stated.

"I know. It definitely doesn't feel good to hear them speak that way. But I know why I'm in a relationship with Sean, and I'm confident he knows why as well." Declan smiled at me.

"I do." I squeezed his knee.

The Donnelleys' chef came in, and judging by the sheepish look on her face, she'd heard everything. "Dinner is ready."

"Thank you, Cynthia." Patrick stood, and we all followed.

"Declan." Fallon reached out and placed his hand on his friend's shoulder. "I hope you know I said nothing bad about you. Faye totally twisted my words."

Declan gave him a side hug. "I know."

"Let's go eat and put this conversation behind us," I offered.

"Sounds like a good plan to me." Rhett grabbed Fallon's hand and pulled him toward the dining room.

I started to walk in the same direction, but Declan stopped me.

"You said you loved me in front of everyone." He beamed.

I couldn't stop the smile that spread across my face. "And I meant it."

27

DECLAN

I stood in Sean's over-the-top kitchen, enjoying the aromas of bacon sizzling in the oven and coffee brewing in the machine as I flipped pancakes on the griddle. Over the last few weeks, we'd spent most nights together at his place, and on the weekends, I cooked us breakfast while he drank his cup of coffee and caught up on world news.

Despite staying together during the week, we still drove to the office separately because we weren't ready to tell everyone at work about our business.

The shit between Luke, his wife, and Emily had gotten wild. After the holiday party, Luke's wife found out about his affair and served him with divorce papers—at work—once everyone had returned to the office following the week-long break. That was enough drama to keep the rumor mill going for a while, and I wasn't ready to be the source of any more.

As I flipped the last pancake, my phone rang. Glancing at the caller

ID, I saw my mom's name flash on the screen. It was a little early for her to be calling, so I was instantly worried.

"Hey, Mom, what's up?" I greeted, trying to keep my tone light.

"Declan ..." Her voice trembled, and I sucked in a breath. "My trailer burnt down."

My heart sank at her words, the spatula in my hand tumbling to the counter. "What? Are you okay? What happened?"

Sean looked up from his iPad and lifted a brow.

"I barely got out in time," she sobbed. "It happened so fast. I don't know what to do."

"Where are you now? Are you hurt?" I quickly turned off the burner and headed to the bedroom for my clothes.

"I'm fine, just ... shaken," she replied between sniffles. "I'm at Virginia's."

Virginia was her neighbor and friend.

"I'll be there as soon as I can, Mom. Just hang tight, okay?" I promised.

"You're coming?"

"Of course I am." I could sense Sean right behind me as I grabbed my jeans off the chair in the corner.

"Okay. I don't know what you can do. Everything is gone," she said, her voice trembling, and I pictured tears streaming down her cheeks.

"We'll figure it out. I'll be there as soon as I can," I repeated to assure her I was on my way.

"Thank you. Love you."

"Love you too."

Ending the call, I tossed the phone onto the bed and stepped into my pants as I spoke to Sean who was standing in the doorway to the bedroom. "I need to go," I said urgently, my mind racing. "My mom's trailer burned down."

"Oh, no!" he gasped and walked toward his walk-in closet. "Is she okay?"

I nodded as I buttoned my jeans. "Yeah, just shaken up, but I need to go and ..." I wasn't sure what I could do, but I knew she and I would both feel better if I was with her and doing whatever I could.

"Of course. I'll drive you," Sean said without hesitation, already grabbing clothes.

"Drive me? Are you sure?"

"One hundred percent. I don't want you getting into a wreck while worrying about her. We'll get you there safely and then see what we can do to help her out."

We. My heart swelled as he used that word.

"Thank you." I grabbed a sweater and threw it on. "I'll go pack up our breakfast and then we can head out when you're ready."

WE WERE MAKING GOOD TIME AS SEAN DROVE THE ESCALADE TOWARD my mom's place. Well, I supposed she no longer had a place, and the thought made me want to crawl into the back seat and cry. Not only was it my mom's home that burned down, but it was mine as well. It was where I grew up. Where I learned to tie my shoelaces. Where I stayed up past bedtime, hiding under the covers and reading books with a flashlight. Where I kissed a boy for the first time while Mom was at work and Tony and I were supposed to be studying for a test. Where Mom and I had so many holidays together and laughter and tears and everything else that came with life.

"You doing okay over there?" Sean squeezed my knee as I looked out the window and remembered things.

"Yeah. Just thinking."

"Whatever needs to happen, we'll make it work."

"I know, but it sucks you're meeting my mom under these circumstances."

"Yeah." Sean blew out a breath. "It's not ideal, is it?"

"I guess I should tell her you're coming too."

"Probably."

I took my phone out of the center console and shot off a text to my mom:

> Sean and I should be there in about an hour

A reply came right away:

> You're bringing Sean?

> He offered to drive

> Wish I had makeup to freshen up

> I think that's the least of our worries. Are you doing okay?

> The best I can. Virginia just made us lunch. We went and got me some clothes at Goodwill a few hours ago

> I'll get us a couple of hotel rooms for the weekend and then we'll figure out something more permanent for you

I had been saving money to buy a new car, but since Sean was still letting me drive the Escalade, getting my own vehicle wasn't pressing.

> You don't need to do that. Insurance will pay for a place for me to stay, or the fire department said they could get me in touch with the Red Cross. Until then, Virginia said I can sleep on her couch

> Not tonight. We're getting you a hotel room at least until other arrangements are made

> Are you sure?

> Absolutely. See you around 3

"Everything okay?" Sean asked as I set my phone back in the cupholder.

"Yeah. But we should find a hotel for the night."

Sean dug into his jeans and pulled out his wallet. "Grab my AMEX."

"You don't need to pay for our rooms," I protested. "You already paid for gas."

"I know I don't need to. I want to."

If Morgan got wind of her father paying for a hotel room for my mother, I wasn't sure what would happen. It was bad enough that she thought I was a gold digger, and she'd probably think my mom was in on some scheme to take Sean's money too.

"At least let me pay for one of the rooms," I argued.

"Declan ..."

"Sean ..."

"Is this about Morgan?"

I lifted a shoulder. "Maybe."

"Christ," Sean muttered under his breath, his fingers drumming lightly on the steering wheel.

I sighed, leaning back into the leather seat. "I just don't know what to do to prove to her that I'm with you because I love you and not because of the amount of money you have in the bank."

Sean shot me a sympathetic glance before returning his gaze back to the road. "Time. Actions speak louder than words, right?"

"Yeah. But lending me your Caddy and now getting us hotel rooms are actions. I don't want to cause more tension between you two."

"She'll come around. We can't let her dictate every decision we make."

"Yeah, but she's your daughter."

He let out a frustrated huff. "She's not the only one who matters here. This is about your mom, Declan. She needs help, and we're going to give it to her, regardless of what Morgan thinks."

Despite my worry, I couldn't help but feel more love for him. "You're right," I admitted, the knot in my chest loosening ever so slightly. "Let's just find a hotel and figure the rest out later."

Hell, maybe Morgan wouldn't even find out.

While Sean drove the rest of the way to my mom's address, I booked us two rooms at a Hilton in town. It wasn't as upscale as I assumed he was used to, but it would have to do.

The Escalade rolled to a stop in front of the charred remains of what used to be my childhood home. The sight of the burnt trailer sent a pang through my chest, and I had to take a moment to steady my breathing before stepping out of the car.

Sean followed suit, and I led the way to where my mom stood in the charred frame of what was once the front door. The smell of burnt plastic hung in the air as we neared, and then my mom turned as we approached, her eyes red-rimmed from tears and exhaustion.

"Declan," she whispered, her voice trembling as she rushed forward to envelop me in a tight hug. "I'm so glad you're here."

I returned the embrace. "Always, and we're going to get through this, I promise."

When we finally pulled apart, my mom's gaze shifted to Sean, who stood a few steps behind me. "And you must be Sean," she said as she extended her hand toward him.

He took her hand gently. "Yes, ma'am. It's nice finally to meet you, although I wish it were under better circumstances."

My mom's eyes welled up with fresh tears, and she nodded. "Thank you for being here for Declan. He's always been my rock, but he needs someone to lean on too."

Sean squeezed her hand reassuringly. "I'll do whatever I can to help."

"Thank you."

"Did anyone figure out what happened?" I asked.

"Fire Marshal Jenkins said the fire started from the lamp in the living room. You know I keep it on every night since I'm alone. I guess something happened with the wiring in it and it sparked a flame. He said he'll have his final report in a few days, but that's what it appears to be."

"That's crazy." I blew out a breath.

"I'm just lucky to have gotten out in time." Fresh tears slid down her cheeks.

I engulfed her in a hug. "Fuck. I'm so happy you did. That had to have been scary."

"You have no idea," she sobbed.

ONCE WE GOT CHECKED INTO THE HOTEL, MOM WENT TO HER ROOM TO shower and change for dinner. We met down in the lobby and headed to the restaurant in the hotel. The clothes Mom had found at Goodwill looked nice; she always could make the best of a small budget.

After we ordered, I couldn't stop thinking about what my mother was going to do. I hated that all of her belongings were just gone. All our pictures. All her clothes. Everything. She'd mentioned her insurance would get her some sort of temporary lodging, but that could be in some roach motel for all we knew.

"Mom," I began, clearing my throat nervously as I glanced up from the menu, "I've been thinking ..."

She looked up, her brow furrowed. "What is it?"

I took a deep breath. "I think ... I think you should move in with me back in Boston."

Her eyes widened in surprise, and for a moment, she was speechless. "Declan, I appreciate the offer. I really do, but I have a job here. I can't just up and leave."

I reached across the table, taking her hand in mine. "Mom, you don't have a place to live, and I'm going to be worried sick about you. I think the diner will understand."

She sighed, her gaze dropping to her lap as she contemplated my words. "I know they would. It's just, I built a life here. I can't just leave."

"Sure you can. We'll be able to see each other every day, and I bet Sam can get you a job at her bar."

"A bar? I don't want to work in a bar," she protested.

"They serve food. It's not like the diner, but it's still a waitressing job."

"I don't know. I've been at the diner for so long. Plus, I'll have temporary lodging soon."

"At some hooker motel, I'm sure."

"We don't know that," she argued.

"If I could interject," Sean said. "I think your work would understand that you need some time off to handle things. As a boss, I wouldn't bat an eye if one of my employees needed to take a few days after their house burned down. Declan can stay with me if you just want to come back to Boston with us and take a few days to clear your head."

"Thank you," I mouthed to him.

He gave me a small nod.

Mom thought it over for a few moments and then said, "All right. But only until I get my temporary lodging."

I scoffed. "Only if it's not some motel with rats and I approve."

"There won't be any rats or hookers." She rolled her eyes.

"You don't know that," I protested.

"We'll see."

28

DECLAN

Monday morning, I called my mom before leaving Sean's place to make sure she was doing okay. I knew she was an early riser since she usually worked the morning shift at the diner.

"Morning, sweetheart," she answered.

"Hey. Just checking in before I head into the office."

"All is good here. Sam and I have decided to go shopping for clothes later once she wakes up."

"That's awesome. I'm glad you two are getting to spend some time together."

"You know I've always loved her."

"I know." I smiled. "Before I run, I have my first hearing on Wednesday. Maybe you'd want to come watch me in action?"

"I would love that."

"Great. I gotta get going. Don't want to be late and piss off the boss." I winked at Sean as he sipped his coffee at the island. Perhaps I wouldn't mind being punished by my boss. "Though I don't think that would be an issue."

"You're right. I'll see you tonight for dinner."

"Sounds good. Have a great day, sweetheart."

"You too."

We hung up and Sean asked, "Ready?"

"Yep."

THE MORNING SUN SPILLED INTO THE PARKING GARAGE AS I PARKED the Escalade beside Sean's Porsche. Stepping out, I glanced over and saw him waiting at the back of his car to walk with me.

"Morning, Declan," he greeted with a smirk.

"Hey, Sean," I replied, mirroring his grin. "Ready for another week?"

Sean chuckled. "Always. Race you to the elevator?"

I laughed. "You're on."

We both took off, laughing as we raced to the elevator. Once we reached it, I pressed the call button as I said, "Damn. Glad you're not this fast in the bedroom."

"Well, well, what do we have here?" a female voice teased.

I turned around quickly, my heart falling out of my chest and I silently prayed she didn't hear what I'd said. "Hey, Camille. Didn't know you were here already."

She sauntered over. "Clearly not. New office romance I should know about?"

I felt my cheeks heat, surprised by her observation. Sean shifted uncomfortably beside me, his usual confidence faltering for a moment.

"Uh, no, it's nothing like that," I stammered, trying to regain my composure.

Her eyes narrowed, her gaze flickering between us. "Are you sure about that?"

Sean cleared his throat. "Yeah, Camille."

"Hmm, well, it certainly seemed like more than that since you mentioned the bedroom."

I looked at Sean and he nodded slowly and then said, "Fine, you caught us. Declan and I are dating."

Camille's eyes widened. "Wait, really?"

I stepped closer to my boyfriend. "Yeah, we are."

A slow grin spread across her face. "Wow, I had no idea."

I scratched the back of my head. "Yeah, it's been a bit of a secret until now."

"But hey, secrets never last long around here, do they?" Sean winked at the office gossiper.

"This is true." I smirked at her. "Plus, Camille, we all know you can't keep a juicy secret to yourself for long." I winked.

She mock-glared at us. "Hey, I resent that! I can be discreet when I want to be."

Sean draped an arm around my shoulders, grinning at her. "Sure, sure. We'll see about that."

With a playful roll of her eyes, she punched me lightly on the arm. "You two are lucky you're so damn cute together."

I chuckled. "Thanks, Camille. And hey, thanks for being cool about it."

"Of course," she replied. "Just promise me one thing."

"What's that?" Sean asked.

She smirked mischievously. "That I get an invite to the wedding."

Sean and I exchanged a look before bursting into laughter. "Deal," I said, still chuckling. "You'll be the first on the list."

As we headed into the elevator, I couldn't help but feel grateful for Camille's support. Maybe the whole office gossip thing wouldn't be so bad after all.

WHENEVER PEOPLE PASSED BY MY DESK IN PAIRS OR GROUPS, I FELT AS though they were whispering about me and Sean. Even though I was okay with the entire office knowing, I still felt a little uneasy. I just wanted to stand on top of my desk and scream at the top of my lungs that I was in love with Sean Ashford and if anyone had a problem, they could kick rocks.

Sliding my chair back, I stood and walked to Sean's office. He was typing away on his laptop, but glanced up and smiled as I approached.

"Hey," he said with a smile.

"I need an afternoon pick-me-up. Want me to bring you back a coffee?"

"I'd love one."

He started to dig into his pocket, and I shook my head.

"I can buy you a coffee."

"Fine." He held up his hands. "Americano, please."

"You got it, Bossman." I winked and turned to grab my coat at my desk.

As I stepped out of the building, the chilly breeze nipped at my cheeks, reminding me that winter hadn't fully loosened its grip on the city yet. I pulled my coat tighter around me and set off toward the coffee shop down the street.

The walk was short, but it gave me a moment to clear my head. As I approached the coffee joint, I noticed someone I recognized standing outside, her focus on the phone in her hands. I hesitated for a moment, debating whether to acknowledge Morgan or simply walk past. But something compelled me to approach her, and try to bridge the gap that had formed between us.

"Morgan," I said, mustering up a smile despite the uneasy knot in my stomach.

She looked up, her gaze meeting mine briefly before darting back to her phone. "Declan," she replied coolly.

She was so engrossed in her phone that she didn't seem to notice the group of rowdy men approaching us on the sidewalk. They swaggered past, their raucous laughter putting me on high alert. As they passed us, one of them let out a low whistle, his gaze lingering on Morgan in a way that made my blood boil, and he called out, "Damn. Nice ass."

I felt a surge of protectiveness wash over me. Without a second thought, I stepped forward, positioning myself between Morgan and the men. "Hey, show some respect," I snapped.

The men paused, their laughter fading as they turned toward us. "What's it to you, pretty boy?" one of them sneered.

"My problem is you acting like a pig," I shot back, my fists clenched at my sides. It wasn't like me to start a fight, but I couldn't *not* do anything when it came to Sean's daughter. She may not trust me, but I loved Sean more than she disliked me.

The men exchanged smirks, clearly amused by my outburst. One of them, the apparent leader of the pack, took a step closer, his eyes narrowed with malicious intent. "You got a mouth on you, huh?"

Before I could respond, Morgan intervened by gripping my arm firmly. "Declan, let's just go inside," she urged.

Reluctantly, I tore my gaze away from the men and followed Morgan's lead, allowing her to guide me toward the coffee shop.

"Yeah, that's what I thought," the one who had taunted me seethed.

Once inside the building, Morgan released her grip on my arm. "Thanks for stepping in, but you didn't need to almost get in a fistfight."

"That guy had no right to talk to you like that," I snapped, unable to shake off the adrenaline coursing through my veins.

She gave me a small smile. "Yeah, well, it's not the first time."

"Still doesn't make it right."

"I know, and thank you."

I blinked. Morgan Ashford said thank you to me? "You're welcome. Can I ... buy you a coffee?"

She snorted. "*You* want to buy *me* a coffee?"

"Yes," I replied. I wanted to say so much more, but at the moment, I knew it would fall on deaf ears.

She stared at me for a beat and then lifted a shoulder. "Okay."

As we stood in line to order, I couldn't keep my thoughts to myself. "Listen, I know you don't exactly trust me, but I want you to know that I care about your dad. A lot."

"Yeah, sure." She rolled her eyes.

I could feel frustration bubbling up inside me, but I pushed it down, determined to stay calm. "Look, I get it. You're just looking out for him, and I respect that. But I'm not some gold digger trying to take advantage of your dad. I love him, Morgan. And I'll do everything in my power to make him happy."

For a moment, there was silence between us. Then, unexpectedly, Morgan let out a sigh, her shoulders slumping ever so slightly. "Fine," she conceded, her voice softer. "Maybe I've been a little too quick to judge."

I couldn't help but feel a surge of relief wash over me. Maybe, just maybe, there was hope for us yet. "Thank you," I said sincerely, offering her a tentative smile. "I promise, I'll do everything I can to prove myself to you."

Morgan nodded, a hint of a smile tugging at the corners of her lips. "I'll hold you to that."

After we got our coffees, we parted ways. She got into a rideshare and I walked back to the office, went straight to Sean's office, and placed the paper cup on the desk in front of him. Then I sat in the chair in front of his desk and took a sip of my vanilla hazelnut latte.

"I ran into Morgan just now."

His eyes widened. "You did? What happened?"

"I think everything is going to work out."

I didn't mean only with Morgan but also with the office knowing we were dating. I had a good feeling that all the pieces were falling into place. Now I just needed to convince my mom to move to Boston permanently.

29

Sean

"Declan, can you come here for a minute?" I called from the doorway of my office.

It was quiet, and I assumed most of the staff had left for the evening, but even when people were around, I no longer cared if they saw me talking to him. We had been the topic of conversation for a few days when word spread that we were together. At least until Emily announced she was pregnant with Luke Nolan's baby. After that, everyone forgot about us because it wasn't as juicy of a story. It seemed as long as cases continued to be assigned on a rotating basis and Declan didn't receive preferential treatment, no one really cared.

"Be right there," he called back.

I moved back to my desk and sat on the edge with my arms crossed over my chest. A few seconds later, he walked in, and his eyes sparkled when he saw me. A couple hours earlier, I'd taken off my suit jacket and tie and rolled up my sleeves. I could only assume he liked the look on me as much as I liked it when he did the same.

"Please tell me my fantasy of getting punished by my boss is finally coming true."

"Anyone out there still?"

He shook his head enthusiastically. "Nope, we're the only two left."

"Maybe you should close the door, just in case."

He swung it closed, locking it for good measure, and then sauntered over to me. When he was within arm's reach, I grabbed his hand and tugged him toward me.

"I've been wanting to fuck you over my desk for a while."

He gasped, and I crushed my lips to his.

"Are you going to let me?" I asked when we finally pulled apart.

"Is that even a question?" He unbuckled his belt and pulled it free in a flourish.

I walked around to the other side of the desk and opened my drawer to retrieve a bottle of lube and a condom.

Declan chuckled. "How long have you had those in there?"

I shrugged. "Since the holiday party."

"The blow job in the supply closet gave you some ideas?" he teased.

"It sure did. Now, put your hands on the desk and don't move."

He spun around and did as I asked. I moved behind him to pull his pants down to his ankles.

"Arch your back for me so I can see you."

He dropped to his elbows and got into position, exposing himself fully to me.

I couldn't wait to bury myself inside of him, but I needed to make sure he was ready because it was going to be fast and hard.

Grabbing the lube, I poured a generous amount on my fingers and circled his hole before pushing two digits inside. When he started pushing back against my hand, I added a third finger and scissored them to make sure I stretched him enough to take me.

"Are you ready for me?" I leaned forward and licked the shell of his ear.

"Uh-huh," he replied breathlessly.

I unbuttoned my pants and pushed them down just far enough to release my cock. While stroking it with one hand, I picked up the condom with the other and used my teeth to rip it open. After rolling the latex down my shaft, I wrapped my hand around the base of my dick and lined myself up to take him.

There wasn't a better feeling in the world than when I sunk deep inside my man.

"Oh god," he moaned.

"I love watching you take all of me." I gripped his hips and began pumping into him.

He reached down between his body and the desk, trying to touch himself, but I pushed his hand away. "I told you not to move."

"Then fuck me harder. I want to come."

Thrusting my hips faster and deeper, I pounded him like he asked. "Is this what you want?"

"Yes," he groaned.

His asshole clenched around me, and that was all it took to send me flying over the edge. As I spilled my release into the condom, I could tell Declan was close to coming as well.

But I didn't want him to finish across my desk.

I wanted him to do it in my mouth.

"Turn around," I directed before kneeling on my office floor.

His eyes widened when he saw me on my knees. "What—"

I knew why he was surprised. Sucking him off was something I hadn't done yet, but I couldn't think of anything I wanted more right then. "I want to taste you."

"If you put your mouth on me, I'm going to come almost immediately."

"That's why I said I wanted to taste you." I winked.

Before he could say anything else, I moved forward and wrapped my lips around his shaft. I couldn't take him as far as he took me, but what I lacked in technique, I tried to make up for with my enthusiasm.

I bobbed up and down, sucking with the same amount of pressure as I enjoyed. Judging by how his fingers tightened in my hair, it was a safe bet I was doing just fine. Adding my hand to the mix, I stroked his length that I couldn't fit into my mouth.

"Sean, I'm going to come," he panted.

I rubbed him a little faster, and when his salty release hit my tongue, I swallowed it down.

Standing, I pressed my lips to his. "I missed you last night."

"I missed you too."

"Come home with me tonight?" I asked as we fixed our clothes.

"Only if we get to do that again."

"Deal."

Since Declan had stayed at his apartment the night before, he'd driven to work. Instead of walking home like usual, I climbed into the Escalade with him, and he drove the few blocks to my place.

"You hungry?" I asked as we rode the elevator up to my floor.

"Starving."

"Jasper made some enchiladas yesterday that I can heat up, or we can order out."

"Enchiladas sound great," he replied as we exited the elevator and walked toward my condo.

I unlocked my door. "Let's grab a quick shower, and then we can eat."

"Sounds good to me."

The shower wasn't quick, but once we were done, we headed to the kitchen, and I pulled out the pan of enchiladas and the beans and rice Jasper had prepared. While those were heating up, I grabbed us a couple of beers.

I handed Declan a bottle and asked, "How was dinner with your mom last night?"

Much to his relief, Tracy had agreed to relocate to Boston, but she'd spent the past two weeks in Pennsylvania tying up some loose ends and helping at the diner while they tried to find her replacement.

She had just gotten back into town the day before, and Declan had been with her instead of coming to my place.

"It was good. She seems happy to be here, and we're going to look at a few apartments this weekend."

"Do you think Sam would let Tracy stay at your place permanently?"

His brow furrowed. "She loves my mom, but we really don't have room for a third person."

"What if you didn't live there?" I took a sip of my beer.

"I don't understand."

"What if you moved in with me?"

His eyes lit up, but then his mouth turned into a frown. "I can't move in with you just because my mom needs a place to live."

"That's not why I'm asking you." I reached across the island and grabbed his hand. "Having you here makes me happy. I want to wake up in the morning and have your face be the first thing I see. The only reason I'm asking is because I love you, and I want to spend as many moments as I can with you."

"I love you too."

"That's not an answer." I smirked.

He laughed. "Of course, I'll move in with you."

The buzzer for the microwave went off, and I pulled out the food. "Man, I'm going to miss this," I said as I plated our food.

"Miss what?"

"Jasper put in his two weeks' notice yesterday."

"Really? Why?"

"His brother's band is going on tour, and they asked him to travel with them as their personal chef."

"That sounds pretty cool, actually."

"Yeah, I can't blame him. He has a chance to travel while doing what he loves. It doesn't get much better than that." I placed his plate in front of him and sat beside him.

He took a bite. "He does make some great food. Wait!" He glared at me playfully. "Did you ask me to move in so I'll cook for you now?"

"I seem to remember you saying I didn't need a chef with you around," I teased.

"I did say that, didn't I?" He laughed and pressed a kiss to my lips. "Maybe I can be your private *naked* chef then."

"I'm not going to say no to that." I winked.

EPILOGUE

Sean

One Week Later

"Is this everything?" I asked as we unloaded a few boxes from the back of Declan's brand-new Kia Sportage parked in the loading zone in front of my building.

Declan had been bringing things to my condo over the past few days, and we hoped to have him fully moved in before the weekend was over.

"Yeah. Once I packed everything, I realized I didn't have that much stuff."

"Hey," Morgan called out as she walked down the street toward us. "Whose car is this?"

I leaned over and kissed her cheek when she reached me since my hands were full. "It's Declan's."

She looked at him. "When did you get a new car?"

"Yesterday. Been saving for a while and it was time." He grinned. "Meet Betsy Junior."

She rolled her eyes. "You named this one too."

"You can't have a car and not name it."

"Sure, you can. It's what most *normal* people do."

"Yeah, but now I can call her BJ." I couldn't stop the chuckle that escaped at Declan's nickname for his new car.

Also, Morgan had been making an effort with Declan since the incident at the coffee shop, and while she was no longer hostile toward him, they now tended to bicker with each other. At least that was preferable to her not wanting to be in the same room as him.

"You want to give us a hand? We can probably make it in one trip if you grab a couple of things." I gave her a pleading smile.

Her eyes widened. "But I just got my nails done."

Declan laughed. "It's fine. I'll come back down and take care of it."

Thankfully, Ryan showed up then. "Hey, you guys want some help?"

"That would be great." Declan handed off the box in his hand and grabbed the remaining items in his trunk.

"What are you guys doing out here, anyway?" I asked as we walked into the lobby. "Don't you usually park in the parking garage?"

"There weren't any spaces left." Morgan pouted. "I had to park in that garage down the street."

"Yeah, I figured your other spot was now reserved for this guy." Ryan nodded at Declan. "So, I parked a couple of blocks away too."

We headed up to my floor. "Well, I'm happy you guys could come over for dinner, even if the parking is super inconvenient," I joked.

Tonight was the first time Declan would join us for our family dinner, and I hoped it was another step toward everyone healing from the hurtful things my kids had said about him.

Once inside my place, we set the boxes down in our bedroom, and then we all gathered around the already set dining table while Jasper put the final touches on what would be the last family meal he made for us.

I poured us all a glass of wine while we waited.

Morgan took a sip and said, "So, now that Declan has a new car, what are you doing with the Escalade?"

"I'm not sure," I admitted. "It's parked at Declan's old place right now. But we can't leave it there for long."

"Sorry to interrupt, but dinner is ready." Jasper came in and placed a platter of pot roast with roasted asparagus and a bowl of mashed potatoes on the table.

"As always, you've outdone yourself," I praised. "We're going to miss you around here, and not just because of the amazing food you serve."

He glanced at Ryan briefly and replied, "I'm going to miss all of you as well. I've enjoyed working here very much."

After one more look at my son, he returned to the kitchen.

"So, about the Escalade," Morgan continued. "I was thinking you should trade it in."

Ryan barked out a laugh. "You were upset because Dad let Declan borrow it, but now you don't want him to keep it?"

"Well, yeah." She shrugged. "It had nothing to do with the vehicle. I just thought he was after our money."

"Gee, thanks." Declan chuckled.

"I don't necessarily feel that way anymore," she huffed. And while she sounded irritated, I didn't miss the slight grin she flashed in his direction.

"Anyway, if you trade in the Escalade, and I trade in my car, we'd have a nice down payment on a BMW M8 I've had my eye on."

"Typical," Ryan muttered, and I could hold back my laugh.

While some things never changed, others kept getting better. Sitting with my boyfriend and my children, sharing a meal, and having a good laugh, I couldn't think of anything better than that.

The End.

ACKNOWLEDGMENTS

We'd like to thank our husbands, Ben and Wayne, who help make sure everything is running smoothly when we are locked away writing. Laura Hull, Virginia Carey, Dan Jenkins, Stacy Nickelson, Geissa Cecilia, and Margaret Neal, thank you for the time you took to help us with this story. We are grateful to each of you.

To Give Me Books Promotions, Tracy Ann, our street team, all the bloggers, and authors who participated in our cover reveal, review tour, and our release day blitz: thank you! We appreciate you helping us spread the word about *our* Off the Bench Duet.

And to all of our readers: thank you for the support you continually show us. Because of you, we are able to pursue our writing dreams.

ALSO BY KIMBERLY KNIGHT AND RACHEL LYN ADAMS

Off the Field Duet – A MM Baseball Romance

Dibs - A MM Friends to Lovers Romance Standalone

Forbidden Series - A MM Forbidden Romance Series

Off the Bench Duet - A MM Hockey Romance

Butcher - A MMF Hockey Romance

ALSO BY KIMBERLY KNIGHT

Club 24 Series – Romantic Suspense

The Chase Duet - Spin off duet from Club 24 - Contemporary Romance

Halo Series – Contemporary Romance

Saddles & Racks Series – Romantic Suspense

Ex-Rated Gigolo – Spin off standalone for Saddles & Racks Series - Romantic Suspense

Sensation Series – Erotic Romance

Reburn – Spin off standalone for Sensation Series - Romantic Suspense

Amore – Spin off standalone for Sensation Series - Romantic Suspense

Dangerously Intertwined Series – Romantic Suspense

Burn Falls – Paranormal Romance Standalone

Lock – Mafia Style retelling of Rapunzel

Deliverance – Spin off standalone for Lock - Mafia Romance

Off the Field Duet – A MM Baseball Romance

Dibs - A MM Friends to Lovers Romance Standalone

Forbidden Series - A MM Forbidden Series

Off the Bench Duet - A MM Hockey Romance

Butcher - A MMF Hockey Romance (Coming Soon)

Audio Books

ALSO BY RACHEL LYN ADAMS

Desert Sinners MC Series
Mac
Colt

Off the Field Duet
Traded
Outed

Forbidden Series
After Hours Lectures
Secrets We Fight
Boss of Attraction
Taste of Surrender

Off the Bench Duet
Hooking the Captain
Retaking the Shot

Standalone
Dibs
Falling for the Unexpected
Butcher (Coming Soon)

ABOUT KIMBERLY KNIGHT

Kimberly Knight is a USA Today Bestselling author who lives in the Central Valley of California with her loving husband, who is a great *research* assistant, and young daughter, who keeps Kimberly on her toes. Kimberly writes in a variety of genres, including romantic suspense, contemporary romance, erotic romance, and paranormal romance. Her books will make you laugh, cry, swoon, and fall in love before she throws you curve balls you never see coming.

When Kimberly isn't writing, you can find her watching her favorite reality TV shows, including cooking competitions, binge-watching true crime documentaries, and going to San Francisco Giants games. She's also a two-time desmoid tumor/cancer fighter, which has made her stronger and an inspiration to her fans.

www.authorkimberlyknight.com

ABOUT RACHEL LYN ADAMS

Rachel Lyn Adams is a USA Today bestselling author who lives in the San Francisco Bay Area with her husband, five children, and a crazy number of fur babies. She writes contemporary and MC romance.

She loves to travel and spend time with her family. Whenever she has some free time, which is rare, you'll find her with a book in her hands or watching reruns of Friends.

www.rachellynadams.com

Made in the USA
Columbia, SC
06 February 2025